W9-AYP-531

A
Harlequin
Romance

OTHER
Harlequin Romances
by GWEN WESTWOOD

Many of these titles are available at your local bookseller,
or through the Harlequin Reader Service.

For a free catalogue listing all available Harlequin Romances,
send your name and address to:

HARLEQUIN READER SERVICE,
M.P.O. Box 707, Niagara Falls, N.Y. 14302
Canadian address: Stratford, Ontario, Canada.

or use order coupon at back of book.

PIRATE
OF THE SUN

by

GWEN WESTWOOD

HARLEQUIN BOOKS   TORONTO
WINNIPEG

Original hard cover edition published in 1972
by Mills & Boon Limited, 17 - 19 Foley Street,
London W1A 1DR, England

© Gwen Westwood 1972

SBN 373-01638-7

Harlequin edition published November 1972

Printed in Canada

1638

CHAPTER ONE

'ARE you coming my way today?' Julie asked, shivering in her scanty scarlet bikini. 'We'll have to start back now. That wretched house has taken the sun early as usual.'

Sandra, in an equally brief blue swimsuit, looked ruefully at the deepening shadow on the little beach that had been bathed in warm sunlight just a little while ago.

'We can't enjoy our late bathe as we used to. It's too bad,' she complained.

'Why don't you come down in the mornings? There are always lots of super chaps here from amongst the holiday people. Most of them go fishing in the afternoons.'

Sandra smiled. It was all very well for Julie, who could spend the whole day on the beach if she wished. In fact the lovely matt golden skin which went so well with the silky black hair and dazzling green eyes showed plainly that this was what she did.

'You have a one-track mind, Julie,' she declared, her large brown eyes twinkling. She ran a comb quickly through her shoulder-length hair that was streaked honey gold where it had been bleached by the sun. 'I'm not a lady of leisure like you. It takes me most of the day to help Aunt Vi run Wave Crest. This hour in the late afternoon is the only time I can spare for a dip.'

'I'd go mad if I couldn't get to the beach more often than that,' said Julie. 'I even get peeved when I have to help Mum occasionally in her boutique. It would be nice, of course, to be able to earn some money. What I would like is an evening job, something glamorous with short hours. Honestly, Sandra, you lead a dog's life. What's the use of struggling on with that little boarding house, now that this super new hotel has been built and all those chalets for families? You should persuade your aunt to retire. It's not as if you have any exciting men coming to the place. Nothing but stodgy family parties wanting a bargain holiday.'

'It's a family hotel,' Sandra admitted. 'It caters for little middle-class people. Not important but nice.'

'Oh, phooeey!' scoffed Julie with the candour of an old friend. 'Mum was saying the other day that that kind of place is outdated now. Even ordinary families want somewhere more modern. Look at those cabanas that the new company have built right near the beach. More families are choosing that kind of holiday. The hotel of course is something else again, the last word in luxury. Craig Ransom must be some kind of million-aire to be able to afford to build the hotel and that house as well. I wish I could see inside the house some time. They say it has everything.'

'Well, it certainly takes up enough room and throws a long shadow,' Sandra said.

By now the whole beach was covered in a blue shade cast by the Moorish palace type of villa built high above the sea upon the ridge.

'Let's go,' said Julie. 'I'm frozen.'

'I think I'll take the path up through the bush,' Sandra replied. 'Goldie will enjoy the run.'

She called to the golden spaniel, who, released from his task of guarding their towels and belongings, was now chasing small fleet-footed wading birds along the water's edge, with more hope than success.

'See you tomorrow, then.' And Julie ran quickly to join the crowd of bathers who were making their way back along the beach in the other direction.

Sandra began to climb the steep sandy path up from the beach. She had wrapped her scanty towel around the bottom half of her blue bikini costume so that it formed a kind of skirt. It was hardly elegant, but it would counteract the coolness of her damp costume. Why hadn't she brought her bathing wrap? Because she had forgotten as usual about the effect of the house and had not expected the sun to vanish so soon. These sunlit May days in Africa were always gorgeous, yet often when the sun dropped low there was a startling change from warmth to an autumn chill.

A path had been bulldozed through the quiet woods, a wide gash bordered by the white splinters from battered trees. This had formed a route for the lorries bringing all the expensive building materials that had gone into the making of the villa and the enormous new hotel that had sprung up it seemed so quickly and looked like some white cliff further along the shore.

Sandra had lived here with her aunt since she was a small girl, her own parents having been killed in an air crash before she was old enough to recollect anything about them. But she remembered what a lovely spot Fair Waves had been before all the new building took place, for this had only happened during the last few years.

Just a while ago, it seemed, the seaside village had been a huddle of small holiday cottages with a couple of hotels that catered in a simple way for families. The golden beach that she had just left had been beautifully lonely, backed by wild banana trees and tangled bush with its sudden sweet-smelling wafts of scented

7

blossom, frequented by birds which seldom showed themselves but made their presence known by the piercing sweetness of their calls.

But now in her opinion the lovely little beach had been spoiled by the presence of that pretentious place like a Moorish palace built for his own use by Craig Ransom, the same man who had been responsible for all the other development. It was he who had supervised the A-frame chalets that seemed to march over the landscape above the beach where once there had been only the lighthouse. And it was he who had directed the building of the great cliff of a hotel, with its five different rooms for eating and entertainment, ranging from the small intimate seafood restaurant where you could listen to folk music, the Chinese one decorated in jade, gold and Mandarin red, the Indian curry place where the waiters wore white turbans and striped gowns, to the more formal restaurant for every kind of gourmet eating and the discothèque where pop music reigned.

And with this development Fair Waves had quickly changed from a sleepy pleasant seaside village that was only crowded during the Christmas and Easter holidays to a swinging sophisticated holiday resort to which wealthy visitors flocked from all over South Africa, from wealthy farmlands and from the big industrial towns on the Reef.

Since the visitors and the owners of the new hotels were able to pay maximum prices, the cost of living had increased by leaps and bounds, so it had become increasingly difficult for Aunt Vi and Sandra to run their boarding house at a reasonable profit, and besides this fewer people came to them. As Julie had said, people these days wanted something more modern.

But Sandra had put all these worries behind her when she came out for her afternoon swim. It was the one pleasure that she tried to keep in spite of the fact that a great deal of the supervision of the African staff and catering was her responsibility.

It was very quiet and peaceful in the woods. From here she could not even see the huge white mass that was Craig Ransom's palace. She had never met him and even Julie, enterprising as she was about meeting new males, had only seen him from a distance.

'He's an absolute dream,' she had declared to Sandra. 'Tall and dark and. . . .'

'Handsome, I suppose,' laughed Sandra. 'Sounds a bit boring.'

'No, not exactly handsome,' Julie replied quite seriously. 'He doesn't look like a business executive, more like some kind of pirate who has dressed himself up in very well cut clothes. He has a hard look, though, that goes with the business bit, steely grey eyes, and, oh, Sandra, he has the most gorgeous lock of dark hair that falls forward over his forehead.'

'Only one?' teased Sandra. 'Has he lost the rest?'

'No, stupid, he still has lots and I'll swear it's still his own. He's old, of course, at least thirty-five, I would say. They say he likes women, but not to marry. He's been married once. All the same, I'd give anything to meet him.'

'I wouldn't,' said Sandra. 'Although he probably doesn't know we exist, he's the cause of all our troubles lately. We can't get enough staff because he takes them all for his hotel, and our food bills have rocketed because his hotel people pay top prices all the time. No, I don't want to meet Craig Ransom. It's true he's a pirate. He's taken away lots of things from us as well as the sun on our beach.'

It wasn't just a question of money, she reflected as she walked along the road through the woods. The change this development had made was devastating. Under the onslaught of progress, the charm of the coast was disappearing together with its wild life. Even in these woods the birds were silent now.

But just as she was thinking this, she heard the distinctive drumming call of a loerie, the lovely shy bird with the green wedge-shaped head, and the next moment she was delighted to see the red flash underneath its wings as the bird swooped across the path, with its dazzling plumage of iridescent green and blue radiant against the dark foliage of the trees.

It perched upon a low branch and she called softly to Goldie, who was running ahead, his long golden ears streaming behind him. She wanted to get as near as possible to the loerie without disturbing it. Oh, it was beautiful with its crested head, intelligent bright eyes and sheeny feathers! But just as she was watching the bird with delight, there was a roaring sound from beyond the curve of the path and a Land-Rover came tearing along, shattering the quietness with the noise of its juggernaut progress.

With a last glimpse of red under-plumage, the bird was gone. Goldie, who had been watching it alertly, ran across the path right in front of the approaching vehicle. Sandra called loudly, but the noise of the engine drowned her shouts. However, the driver, seeing the dog, swerved violently, braking wildly, and ended with the Land-Rover tilted into the soft earth at the side of the path at a most precipitous angle.

Leaving it there, he got out and strode across to Sandra. Even though she had never met him before, she could not fail to recognize him from Julie's description. Yes, the black lock of hair hung over his forehead and his eyes were the steely grey of pewter complementing the hard jaw and dark brows. But today he was dressed in a casual safari suit, its square cut emphasizing the breadth of his shoulders and the slim length of his body. Well, Julie might have been charmed by his appearance, but Sandra found nothing to fascinate her in the frowning regard she had to face.

'Why the hell don't you keep that animal under proper control?' he demanded.

Sandra considered rapidly whether she should speak to him at all, but then felt so furious that she was incapable of making a silent, dignified retreat.

'I don't expect traffic in the middle of these woods,' she said. 'My dog has a perfect right to be off the leash here.'

'It can't have much brain if it dashes in front of a vehicle like that. But I suppose in a small place like this you can't expect animals to have traffic sense.'

Sandra was still trembling from the shock of the sudden incident. Goldie was very precious to her and accompanied her everywhere she went. How dared this wretched, arrogant man criticize her and the dog and even the village! It was his fault that the traffic had increased and their peace had gone even in these woods.

'Dogs in Fair Waves didn't need traffic sense until you and your company started all this development, Mr. Ransom!' she declared hotly.

A smile flickered over his face. It seemed to transform his hard expression and for the first time he looked her up and down appraisingly. She was very conscious of the fact that she was wearing merely her blue bikini and a small towel. Oh dear, I wish I were properly dressed, she thought. It's difficult to be dignified in a brief swimsuit.

'So you know who I am?' he asked. 'There you have the advantage of me. I haven't met you before, have I? I never forget a pretty face.' His grey eyes slid briefly downwards to the honey-gold shoulders, the blue bikini top and tanned midriff. 'Or figure,' he added, smiling now with a glint of mischief.

I suppose this kind of practised charm would fascinate Julie, Sandra thought, but it certainly cuts no ice with me.

'No, Mr. Ransom,' she replied coolly. 'You've never met me before, nor are you very likely to meet me again.'

'In that case let me offer you a drink to prolong our one and only meeting. You look as if you need it. I'll soon have this junk wagon out of the sand and we can be at the house in a couple of minutes.'

It was an opportunity that Julie would have given anything to have, but Sandra was not impressed.

'Thank you, Mr. Ransom, but I have work to do. In any case I couldn't. . . .'

Even when he smiled there was a wicked glint about the grey eyes.

'You needn't be scared, I assure you. I have a large domestic staff who sometimes chaperon me a little too much for my taste. It's almost impossible to be alone in that house.'

'Certainly I'm not scared, but I just haven't the time to spare, Mr. Ransom.'

'Nor the inclination, it seems. Come now, let me make up for my first words to you. I'm not in the habit of being rude to attractive strangers. I promise I'll run you back to wherever you have to go. Do come.'

Sandra hesitated. It would be fun to be able to tell Julie about it and she was awfully cold and still had a long way to walk back. It would be comforting to have a hot drink and be driven back before she started the rather arduous chores of the little hotel.

'Very well,' she consented. 'I'll come, but it will only be for a very short time.'

Craig Ransom smiled delightedly.

'That's grand. We'll see about the short time when we get there. I'm not used to taking no for an answer.'

Sandra now rather regretted that she had consented to go. If it would have been a new experience for Craig Ransom to be refused, she wished she could have been the one to give it to him. He quickly righted the Land-Rover and it seemed none the worse for the mishap. As he helped her up the high steps he took her arm.

'Why, you're frozen, my dear. Here, take my jacket.'

Before she could protest he had stripped off his safari coat and wrapped it around her.

'But you ... you'll be cold,' she stammered, somewhat embarrassed by the close proximity of this determined man who was sitting in the driver's seat seemingly unconscious of his deeply tanned body that he had now bared to the waist.

'In this climate!' he laughed. 'It's only a couple of months since I was working in northern Canada. You don't expect me to feel cold here, do you?'

Sandra huddled into the jacket that was still warm from his wearing it. It felt very comforting and smelled very masculine with a combination of some expensive after-shave lotion and the fragrance of good cigars.

'You don't realize how honoured you are, my dear,' said Craig. 'Very few people have seen my house. I like to preserve a little privacy in my personal life at least.'

At close quarters the house was even more imposing than it had appeared from the beach. A sweeping drive surrounded a lawn that was already like green velvet. Sandra realized that a small fortune must have been spent to achieve such a result in so short a time. The bougainvilleas, flaunting their laden branches of scarlet clustered flowers, and the petrea, deep purple against the chalk-white walls, must have been planted here while in full bloom. Cineraria, purple, mauve and pink, stood high upon the shady banks together with bright-leaved coleus.

They had scarcely halted when an African servant in red fez and white uniform was opening the great studded door and another servant in maroon livery had commandeered the Land-Rover and was driving it towards the block of garages upon the left.

This house had obviously been built with the summer season in mind. The hall was beautiful, but the marble pavement, the mosaic murals of fish and dolphins and the fountain cascading over natural rocks and green with ferns did nothing to dispel Sandra's discomfort. She had slipped out of Craig's jacket, not liking to keep it any longer, and now she felt very cold and yearned to be back in the boarding house having a hot bath. I'm quite frozen. Why did I come? she thought.

'Would you like whisky or brandy or wine, or would you prefer hot chocolate?' Craig was asking.

'Hot chocolate would be lovely.'

He conveyed his orders through a speaking tube and directed her down some marble stairs into a large sitting-room, with Goldie running ahead nonchalantly as if he enjoyed leaving muddy footprints in such luxurious surroundings.

The house had been built in sloping terraces, for the site was very precipitous and had been hacked out of the hillside that sloped down to the beach. The sitting-room was huge with enormous windows beyond which the Indian Ocean pulsed and sparkled in a vast expanse of dark blue with small white-crested waves.

The floors were of dark red tile but covered by exquisite Persian rugs in jewel-like colours, and there was a log fire, Sandra was thankful to observe, the fire-irons and bars of gleaming silver. In this part of the room there was a large shaggy cream carpet and the settees and chairs were covered with deep emerald velvet.

'Are you still cold?' asked Craig, as Sandra was drawn irresistibly to the fire. 'We must do something about that.'

He touched the tapestry bell pull suspended beside the door. In a few moments the door was opened silently and a servant was given directions to bring a wrap for Sandra.

Meanwhile Sandra was examining the portrait above the fireplace. It was a modern picture of a girl, aged about twelve. Not a beautiful face but striking. A dark child with the same grey eyes and defiant tilt to the head that distinguished the man at Sandra's side. But whereas Craig, judging from his expression, had conquered the world about him, the young girl behind her defiance had a wistful expression and there was something touching about her in spite of the too sophisticated hairdo and modern expensive clothes.

'My daughter Kim,' said the vibrant voice behind her. 'At a difficult age, I'm afraid. Neither a child nor a woman.'

'She has an interesting face,' Sandra commented, thinking, I should like to meet her to see what she's really like.

She was unaware that Craig was standing so close behind her and when he put his hands on her shoulders she started. His hands slid down her arms, vibrantly warm against her cool skin.

'Are you warmer now?' he asked.

But before she could reply or slip from his grasp, the door opened and a young girl appeared there. Obviously this was the original of the portrait. Craig's hands fell to his sides, but Kim had seen them together and evidently put her own interpretation upon the scene. Her face held a knowing look of contempt, an ugly expression for so young a child.

'Francine asked me to bring a robe,' she said in a sulky tone.

Craig's face lit up. He seemed completely unaware of his daughter's mood, or if he was aware of it he ignored it.

'This is Kim,' he said, putting his arm around her, as if announcing, 'This is my dearest jewel.'

She shrugged away from his touch.

'And this is . . .' then Craig laughed. 'I'm so sorry. I don't seem to know your name.'

'It's Sandra Hamilton.'

Not that it's of any importance to you, Craig Ransom, Sandra thought, for I certainly mean to avoid you in future. This is our first and last meeting, I hope. She slipped on the proffered robe, a silk affair of blue and violet stripes, as if to hide the place where she could still feel the pressure of those warm sunburned hands upon the smooth curve of her shoulders.

The servant who had opened the front door now entered with a tray upon which were a silver jug of steaming chocolate and a plate of small sugared cakes.

'There's a trunk call coming through from London, Mr. Ransom,' he said. 'Will you take it here or in the study?'

'The study, Benson. Will you excuse me for a few minutes, Miss Hamilton? Doubtless Kim will entertain you.'

Kim, having helped herself to a cake without offering one to Sandra, was sitting upon a brown and cream gilded leather camel stool. On her father's departure, she looked up and stared rather rudely.

'How did you meet Craig?' she asked abruptly.

Sandra, sipping her hot chocolate gratefully, reflected that it seemed somehow suitable that his daughter called him Craig. She could not imagine any affectionate name such as Daddy being used for him.

'I met him in the woods near the house,' she replied. 'I'd been bathing.'

Kim laughed without mirth.

'It's fantastic the way girls try to meet Craig,' she informed Sandra. 'They'll do anything to get to know him, but they don't usually manage to get him to bring them to the house.'

'Really?' said Sandra coldly. She felt annoyed and irritated with the child and wanted to assure her that she did not care whether she ever saw Craig again, but did not quite dare.

'Yes, girls who want to get taken on at the hotel as dance hostesses or entertainers go to all kinds of lengths to appear in front of him when they're wearing a bikini or sometimes even less. Are you trying to get a job at the hotel?'

'No,' said Sandra, emphatically. 'I help my aunt run a hotel here. I certainly don't want to do any other work.'

'Which hotel does your aunt have?'

'Wave Crest.'

'Heavens, you could scarcely call that a hotel, could you?' exclaimed Kim, rudely. 'It's just an old boarding house. When I first came here I thought with all those round buildings that it was like an African village. Craig said he wondered how anyone could be bothered to keep it going.'

Sandra did not think this criticism merited a reply. What a dreadful child! And yet there was something hurt and sensitive about the too large mouth. She was quite plain except for those huge beautiful grey eyes. And dressed in far too grown-up a manner.

'Craig has hundreds of girls in love with him, but he never really cares about any of them. He gets tired of them very quickly. He says most women are pretty boring on the whole.'

'I don't think your father would like you to discuss these things with a stranger, Kim, do you?'

The child shrugged her shoulders and opened her beautiful eyes wide.

'He wouldn't care. You don't think he cares what anyone thinks of him, do you? He just does what he likes always. And when I grow up, I'm going to be like that too. Of course I'll be able to because I'll have lots of money and beautiful clothes.'

'But, Kim . . . .' said Sandra a little helplessly. What could she say? The whole of this luxurious house was a tribute to the materialism and selfishness that this child was preaching. What a terrible way to bring up a daughter! Her feelings towards Craig hardened even more, if that were possible.

When he came back into the room, she rose and said in a decided manner, 'I must go now, Mr. Ransom. Please don't bother about driving me home. I can easily walk.'

His well-defined dark eyebrows rose in a quizzical tilt.

'I wouldn't dream of letting you go home alone, Miss Hamilton. Just one moment while I ring for the car.'

'May I come with you, Craig?' Kim asked. The pose of ultra-sophistication seemed to have been dropped and she sounded like an eager child.

'Not this time, Kimmy. Why not go and change into something smashing? For once I have time to have dinner with you tonight.'

The child's face lit up, though she had flashed a look of dislike at Sandra when she had been forbidden to come.

'Oh, super! You do promise? You won't decide to have dinner with her, will you?'

Craig laughed. 'Maybe some other time if I can persuade her.'

In the driveway a maroon Jaguar was waiting.

'I'll drive myself,' Craig informed the waiting chauffeur.

Sandra sat in silence while he negotiated the steep driveway. How effortlessly the powerful car responded to his touch! She sighed, thinking of her struggles with her aunt's old bulky saloon car that was used for everything from transporting summer visitors from the station in the nearest town to carrying market produce.

'Why the large sigh? I'm sorry I've proved such poor company. We'll have to try to remedy that.'

Sandra glanced at the rugged face of the stranger beside her and seethed inwardly with indignation. From the things Kim had told her it seemed he thought himself irresistible to women and probably he considered them easy game. She wished she had had time to be very freezing towards him when he had started to touch her. Probably she would never get another opportunity, for it was hardly likely they would meet again. Their lives were lived in very different channels.

From the high ridge along which they were driving, she could see the sun setting beyond the distant hills and to the right the beach had disappeared below the wine-dark sea. Lights glittered like diamonds in the great cliff of Craig Ransom's hotel, but, as they approached the tangled bush surrounding the small lawn of her aunt's boarding house, there was the warm golden glow of oil lamps. Although electricity had been installed with the new development, her aunt still preferred to keep a few of the old lamps.

'Please stop here, Mr. Ransom. There's no need to come further. I must rush away because the chef finds it difficult to cope with the dinner on his own.'

She tried to open the door of the car, but found it was locked and the intricacies of the catch defeated her. Craig smiled lazily.

'I don't approve of independent woman who open their own doors.' he said. 'I like to keep them waiting. Just a minute, Miss Hamilton.'

He leaned towards her and she thought he intended

to open the car door from the inside, but instead he put his arm around her.

'Too bad we were interrupted before,' he said with a very charming smile. 'Has anyone ever told you how sweet you are?'

His other hand caressed her cheek, then turned her face towards him, so that she was only inches away from the confident tilt of his lips and his wicked laughing eyes.

'Too bad you've found someone who doesn't need anything from you, Mr. Ransom,' she said coldly.

'And what do you mean by that?' he asked. The smile had gone, but he still held her tightly so that it was impossible to get away.

'I've been told that most girls to whom you make love want something from you, usually a place in your hotel organization. What a way to have to use to gain favours, Mr. Ransom!'

His arm dropped from her shoulders and he released his grasp upon her chin.

'That's a diabolical thing to say, Miss Hamilton! I knew I had a bad reputation, but it's never been brought home to me quite so forcibly before. Tell me, who told you this?'

Sandra was silent. She dared not say that the story came from his own young daughter.

'So in your opinion women are only willing to let me make love to them if I'm prepared to grant them some favour?'

'So I understand.'

'Take care, Miss Hamilton. I don't take offence easily, but when I do the people who hurt me are usually sorry.'

'I don't care for your threats any more than your

lovemaking, Mr. Ransom. Besides, our lives are lived very far apart. As I said before, I hardly expect to meet you again.'

She made a move to get out of the car and at last he opened the door for her, but got out himself and stood beside her.

'Good-bye, Mr. Ransom,' she said quickly. 'Thank you for the lift.'

But he caught her hand and held her again in that hard grasp.

'Oh, you South African girls! You're always dressed so provocatively, but it seems only the sun is allowed to make love to you!'

They were interrupted by Aunt Violet who came running down the path, quite unaware of the fact that to Sandra at that moment she looked like a guardian angel, a short, tubby angel with flyaway silver hair apparently made of spun silk, vividly blue eyes and a rosy brown face the colour of a late autumn apple.

'Oh, it's you, Sandra! How silly of me. When I heard a car stop I thought it was the man about the freezer.'

She gave Craig the kindly incurious blue gaze with which she accepted everyone.

'This is Craig Ransom,' said Sandra. 'He gave me a lift home.'

'How kind of you, Mr. Ransom. It's a long walk for Sandra from the beach and she never gets any rest after it because she has to run around helping with dinner and doesn't even have a chance to sit down. But do come in, Mr. Ransom. Dinner's fairly organized and at least we can offer you a drink after your trouble.'

Sandra was quite sure Craig would refuse, but to her surprise he said he would like to stay.

'You won't mind having it on the stoep near the kitchen, will you?' Aunt Violet stated rather than asked. 'We must keep an eye on Jabulani. He's our chef, but not too expert without a little advice.'

'But, Aunt Vi . . .' Sandra began.

Then she thought, what did it matter? Let Craig see how the other half lived by all means. He had told Kim he wondered how anyone could be bothered to keep the place going. Now this would confirm his ideas when he saw how shabby the interior was.

Aunt Vi ushered them on to the little glassed-in verandah with its old basket chairs and faded curtains with the same aplomb she would have used had she been showing Craig into a salon of priceless antiques.

'Now what can we offer you?' she asked. 'Sandra, we still have that half bottle of brandy we bought for last year's Christmas pudding in my cupboard, haven't we? And there's the sherry we used for the trifle if you would prefer that. It's rather sweet, I'm told. Otherwise I can offer you some of my lemonade made with lemons from my own tree.'

'That would be grand,' said Craig, who, Sandra noticed, had not even smiled at Aunt Vi's suggested drinks.

He sipped his lemonade sedately, and complimented Aunt Vi upon its excellent flavour. Sandra wished impatiently that he would finish it and be gone, but Aunt Vi had launched into a cheerful account of how they managed to run the hotel in spite of lack of funds. Why must she be so expansive about it to Craig Ransom of all people? He could not be in the least interested about their difficulties. He could not possibly be expected even to understand them when he apparently had limitless funds at his disposal.

'And now the freezer has packed up,' Aunt Vi was saying. 'Isn't that unfortunate? Sandra is so good about going herself to get inexpensive cuts of meat at the shops in town. She watches the advertisements for special offers and is very clever about looking for bargains.'

Sandra flushed with embarrassment.

'Aunt Vi, I'm sure Mr. Ransom can't be interested.'

'Ah, but I am, I assure you, Miss Hamilton. Anything connected with hotel catering interests me. You know it's my business too.'

She thought he must be making fun of her. How could he compare his hotel with theirs? She was quite glad when they were interrupted by Jabulani, even though he was dressed in his oldest uniform that had been patched over and over again.

'Miss Sandra, big trouble. Fish smell bad. Freezer gone sick. What cook for second course? Peoples have spaghetti and mince twice already this week.'

'I'll come, Jabulani,' said Sandra, and thankfully saw that Craig had risen to go.

'For the second time, good-bye, Miss Hamilton,' he said, smiling slightly as if remembering her previous indignation.

'No one calls her Miss Hamilton, Mr. Ransom. Her name is Sandra, and I'm Aunt Vi to everyone,' said Vi.

'That's grand. Good-bye, Sandra. Thanks for the drink, Aunt Vi. And you must call me Craig.'

'That's a good name. I like it. Come again, Craig, when you have the time.'

'I certainly will do that,' said Craig, charming Aunt Vi with his vivid smile.

'What a pleasant man,' she commented as the purr of the Jaguar died away in the distance.

Sandra said nothing. She felt angry again as she escaped to the kitchen. She wished he had not been so nice to Aunt Vi, who trusted people implicitly and was disappointed if they failed to live up to her opinion of them. What Craig had said held no meaning. He was probably laughing to himself about the whole set-up here. And Sandra felt quite certain that they would never see him here again. But in that she was wrong.

CHAPTER TWO

SATURDAY morning was always rushed. People came for a drive from the large seaside resort a few miles down the coast and found it pleasant to bring their children to the small tea-garden attached to Wave Crest, with its modest collection of animals and birds which provided an additional attraction together with a couple of rather worn swings and slides.

Serving teas was an added chore on top of planning the week-end meals for the hotel, but in the present situation Sandra and Aunt Vi found it necessary to earn every added sum they could, however small.

Sandra had been up since dawn baking scones and whipping cream for the cream scones with jam or the crumbly apple pie with cream that their customers expected. Now at ten-thirty she seemed to have reached a peak of activity with the young African boys who served as waiters on a Saturday rushing into the hot kitchen to state their orders and the loaded trays to arrange besides the task of keeping the urns going full of boiling water and the replenishment of supplies of food.

Wearing a brief pair of shorts and yellow halter-necked top for coolness in the hot kitchen, Sandra was not too pleased when Gary came in to interrupt her. He was a young newspaper reporter who worked for the journal in the nearby town and stayed at the hotel, but his claim to fame at the present time was that he seemed to be Julie's favourite boy-friend. His bright red head and freckled face peered around the kitchen door and he looked at the chaotic scene, then slid the rest of his long thin body into an available space, took a slice of chocolate cake from a tray and proceeded to eat it as if he had not had food for a week.

'You look busy this morning,' he commented as he was nearly knocked flying by one of the hurrying waiters.

'That's the understatement of the year,' Sandra said. 'If you intend to stay here, Gary, you could butter these scones.'

'O.K., if you promise me I can hear the phone from here. I'm expecting a call from Julie. She was to confirm our arrangement for this evening.'

'Why don't you phone her?'

'Forbidden. I'm hoping to make Julie love me, but her mama doesn't agree. She thinks Julie should capture some rich young man. She doesn't intend that her daughter should marry a struggling newspaperman.'

Could Julie love him? Sandra had known Julie since they were at school together and in the last few years she had believed herself in love with more men than Sandra could count or remember. But she always assured Sandra that she was searching for her ideal man and when she found him everything would be different. But was Gary that man? Sandra could not quite believe so. But perhaps she was not being fair to her friend. Gary, though not exactly good-looking with his flaming red hair, freckled face and long sunburned frame, was good company, lively and amusing with the quick mind that would probably take him far in the newspaper world.

She brushed a damp lock of hair from her forehead. She was far too busy to think about Gary and Julie's feelings for him, sentimental or otherwise. The important question at the moment was whether there would be enough apple pie to last the morning.

The phone rang in the small hallway near the kitchen. Gary brightened visibly and rushed away, but was back in a few seconds looking rather crestfallen.

'It's for you,' he told Sandra. 'Moving in high circles lately, aren't you?'

'What do you mean?' asked Sandra.

'Wait and see if you don't know,' said Gary cryptically.

'Don't be like that. Please tell me.'

'Craig Ransom. Low thrilling voice.'

Gary imitated it, rolling his eyes in a fine romantic frenzy and putting his arms around Sandra.

'Miss Hamilton ... or can I call you Sandra? I'm wanting a manageress for my new hotel and I hear you're just the girl for me.'

'Stop fooling and let me go, Gary.'

Gary was wrong in one thing. He called her Sandra straight away. The voice was low and persuasive, but it depended how willing you were to be thrilled, she thought.

'Sandra, I enjoyed meeting you and your aunt yesterday. I've phoned to ask if you would be able to use a freezer that's been discarded in favour of a later model but is still in working order.'

'But, Mr. Ransom. . . .'

'Craig, we agreed, you remember.'

'My aunt couldn't possibly afford the kind of freezer you would have, even if it is second-hand.'

'There's no question of payment, Sandra. I would be grateful if you could give it house-room. You would be doing me a favour by storing it.'

This could hardly be true, thought Sandra. There

must be lots of spare room in that large hotel. She hated the idea of accepting such a favour from this man who had antagonized her from the moment she first saw him. But what a boon it would be for them! She hesitated.

'I'll ask Aunt Vi,' she compromised.

'Do that. But meanwhile I'll send a truck with it. You can send it back if you decide you don't want it.'

Before she could protest he had rung off.

Once more she felt a surge of indignation at his high-handed methods. How dared he think he could patronize them just because he had seen how shabby and rundown their hotel was!

Gary was still lingering within earshot of the phone.

'Do you know this guy well?' he demanded.

'Hardly at all,' Sandra replied. 'And I don't want to know him.'

'What a pity! I thought you might be able to help me. I'm angling for an interview with him. He's hot news around this neighbourhood. I'd specially like to do an article about his house and his home life. No reporter has managed to get into the place yet. He's a bit standoffish where that side of his life is concerned.'

'Sorry, I can't help,' said Sandra. She was certainly not going to tell Gary she had been inside Craig's house.

The morning rush was almost over now and Sandra found Aunt Vi showing her white sulphur-crested cockatoo to an assembly of children.

'What's your name?' she asked the bird.

'Robert,' croaked the bird. Then, not to be outdone

by Aunt Vi, he repeated, 'What's your name ...
Robert.'

The two giant tortoises were lumbering around their
paddock slowly consuming the lettuce provided for
them by admiring children, and a tall blue crane
walked with the rather stilted gait of an old-fashioned
mannequin, its bright eyes peering this way and that in
search of titbits.

'How very kind of Mr. Ransom ... Craig,' said
Aunt Vi, when Sandra had told her about the freezer.
'He seems a very generous man, and so charming.'

She looked speculatively at her niece, but Sandra
chose to ignore this.

'It's all part of his stock in trade,' she said. 'How to
win friends and influence people. Business methods.
You have to be charming in the hotel trade. Even we
know that. Next thing,' she added, 'he'll be wanting to
take over our hotel.'

'What nonsense,' said Aunt Violet briskly. 'He's just
a very kindhearted man and he realized our difficulties
last night. I will certainly accept the loan of the freezer.
One should take things like this in the spirit in which
they're done. That's what I always tell you, Sandra. If
you have faith in life, some way out of your difficulties
always presents itself.'

Sandra thought she might have known Aunt Vi
would take this attitude. But all the same she still felt
nettled.

'Is he bringing it himself?' asked her aunt.

'No, of course not. He's sending it with one of his
minions.'

Aunt Vi looked a little startled at the tone of
Sandra's voice, but at that moment their conversation
was interrupted by a loud 'Yoo-hoo!'

It was Julie arriving in a bright yellow beach buggy. Her brief shorts and tunic were buttercup yellow too and her dark hair was swirled up into a topknot of elegant loops.

She had hardly halted the little vehicle upon the grass when she jumped out and rushed over to Sandra, her green eyes shining with excitement.

'Oh, Sandra, wonderful news! I've heard something absolutely super. They need dance hostesses to work two or three times a week at the new hotel. The pay is terrific and it's just evening work. They're interviewing applicants first thing on Monday morning.'

'What would you have to do?' asked Sandra.

'Help with the discothèque, dance with tired business men, do a bit of go-go dancing ... all that kind of thing. It's money for jam. I adore dancing.'

Gary, homing in like a red setter, as soon as he heard Julie's voice, had emerged from the kitchen premises and joined them. He did not look very pleased with Julie's news.

'You'll have to be careful in a job like that,' he said. 'You might meet all kinds of odd types.'

'At the Casa del Sol? Well, at least they'll be rich types. Better than some of your friends. Some of your newspaper pals are odd bods, you must admit.'

'I'll grant you that,' Gary admitted. 'But all the same, I don't like the sound of this job, Julie.'

'You don't have to like it,' she said. 'No one's asking you to do it. How about it, Sandra? Will you come with me on Monday?'

'Me?' asked Sandra, astonished. 'You aren't suggesting . . .?'

'Why not?' asked Julie. 'You don't have to be there until eight. Even if you have to help with dinner here, you know it's always over by seven-thirty. Wouldn't you like to earn some more money and have fun at the same time? I think it's a great idea. It isn't every night.'

It was true, thought Sandra. It would be good to have extra money. She would be able to help Aunt Vi a bit, even if it was only enough to buy them some new clothes. They had both become rather shabby during the last months. It was only because in this kind of life you needed only cotton dresses, shorts and bathing suits that Sandra was able to manage.

'I wouldn't have anything to wear,' she said. 'Only the old white dress I wear for the do's here.'

'I've got heaps of cocktail dresses I could lend you, or maybe Mum could find something inexpensive in the boutique. They might even provide the clothes.'

'Yes,' said Sandra doubtfully. Julie was distinctly more curvaceous than she was herself. And Julie's mother certainly did not stock anything very inexpensive, as she knew from past experience.

'Anyhow, you can worry about that when you're offered the job,' said Julie practically. 'We have to get it first.'

'All right, I'll come,' said Sandra. Then she had a sudden thought. 'But who will interview us? Will Craig Ransom be there?'

'No such luck. It will be that rather suave manager he has, Manoel de Villiers. Craig Ransom wouldn't be bothered to interview go-go girls. He's far too superior for that, I would say. But we may have a chance to meet him later. We can dream, anyway.'

Sandra had given up her intention of telling Julie about the visit to Craig's house. Julie would be so excited and make a big fuss about it. And although she usually confided in Julie, she was not at all sure that she wanted to talk about Craig Ransom.

Julie and Gary were discussing their plans for that evening.

'What do you say to the drive-in?' asked Gary. 'We can go early and pick up a meal at the snack bar there.'

'Hamburger and coffee,' said Julie. 'I had hoped we would go dancing. I've got gorgeous new emerald velvet hot pants with a slit skirt. Why can't we go to the Starlight Room at the Casa del Sol?'

'On a reporter's pay?' scoffed Gary. 'Be your age, ducky.'

'If I get that job, I'll probably be able to get you in at the back door,' Julie promised.

'But I'd still have to pay for what we ate,' declared Gary. 'No, thank you. We'll have plenty of high living when I write my best-seller, I promise you.'

'It looks as if we'll have to wait a pretty long time for that, I would say.'

Sandra thought it was time to intervene.

'We're having a barbecue on the beach tonight for our guests, followed by a bit of a hop to taped music,' she said. 'If you want to come after the drive-in programme is over, you're welcome.'

'I thought you had Saturday evenings free,' said Julie.'

'I do usually because most people go into town to do a show on a Saturday. But there happen to be a good few people here with children, so we organized a beach picnic for them.'

'You are a demon for work, aren't you, Sandra?' Julie commented. 'Come on, Gary, let's catch a swim before lunch. I suppose there's no hope of persuading you to come, Sandra?'

'No hope at all,' Sandra smiled. 'Though I'd adore one. But I have to go and make macaroni cheese look like something new by garnishing it up with green pepper and tomatoes. It's a bit beyond Jabulani.'

Rather enviously she watched them drive off towards the beach in the yellow buggy. Sandra's black hair streamed behind her in the breeze. She looked absolutely beautiful. Sandra was all at once conscious that her own hair hung in lank wisps upon her shoulders and that she had become covered with smuts from the old coal-stove. She would have a quick shower before lunch as soon as this meal had been organized.

She had just finished her instructions to Jabulani when she was conscious that someone was standing in the doorway of the kitchen. Turning and expecting to see one of the guests, she was surprised to see Craig. He looked very large, clean and competent in a white polo-necked knit shirt and navy shorts, and Kim, who accompanied him, was dressed in a very smart navy sundress with bare midriff, a rather adult outfit that looked very expensive.

Sandra felt conscious of her own dishevelled appearance, but shrugged the thought away. What did it matter to her how she looked to Craig, who was used to seeing most beautiful girls at his hotel? It would make a change for him to see a plain one.

'One freezer for the use of!' Craig announced. 'Where are you proposing to put it? Here in this alcove would be a good place, then it would be quite close to the kitchen without being in the way.'

'Oh, but I don't know whether . . .' she began, but found her protests drowned by Craig's instructions. It

34

was obvious that he was used to giving orders. In no time at all the freezer was installed and he had not even asked whether they had decided in favour of accepting his offer.

After one look at the kitchen, Kim had wandered outside. They found her talking to Aunt Vi.

'Why have you got such a funny hotel?' she was asking.

Aunt Vi considered this gravely.

'By "funny",' she said, 'do you mean funny peculiar or funny ha-ha?'

'Both,' said Kim. 'Why isn't it all in one piece instead of having lots of little huts?'

'Because the Africans in these parts know how to build little huts. They've been building them in the same way for hundreds of years. They're inexpensive, and people like the novelty of sleeping in a round hut, we find.'

'I wouldn't,' declared Kim emphatically. 'You should see my bedroom. I have wallpaper to match the curtains and a bathroom en suite and wall-to-wall carpeting and white furniture.'

'That sounds very fine,' said Aunt Vi. 'But people sleep well in little round huts, I think.'

'Would you like to see the birds and tortoises, Kim?' Sandra asked. Poor Kim! The mixture of sophistication and childishness was rather pathetic. Her plain little face looked sallow above the beautifully cut dark blue sun-suit. And her hair, obviously set at a hairdressers, was in an elaborate topknot of curls, far too grown-up a style for a child of her age.

'If you want to show them to me,' she assented with not much grace.

But Robert's wide vocabulary brought a smile to the

35

small plain face, and the wide grey eyes crinkled as she fed lettuce to the tortoises. She needs to learn to be a child, thought Sandra. She's far too grown-up. But Craig can obviously see nothing wrong. The expression of his face had softened as he regarded Kim with Aunt Vi's pet. He's not all hardness, Sandra thought. He's capable of affection, but not to women in general, certainly. As she saw the expression of his grey eyes change as if sunshine had played upon the steely surface of a lake, she was suddenly surprised to find in herself a brief longing to be the object of such an affectionate glance.

'It's nicer than I thought. Can I come again?' asked Kim.

'Any time,' Aunt Vi said. 'You can help me with cleaning out the cages and pens.'

Kim looked taken aback. 'That's servants' work,' she said. 'I wouldn't know how.'

'Then you could learn,' said Aunt Vi.

'Come along, Kim. We mustn't waste any more of these busy people's time,' said Craig. And with a wave of his hand and a smooth changing of gears he was gone.

'That's a poor little rich girl,' said Aunt Vi. 'We'll have to see what we can do about her.'

'I doubt whether she'll come again. I think you frightened her off. She isn't used to doing chores.'

'We'll see. It's my opinion that the child needs a bit of female company. She obviously gets too much of her own way as well as of everything else in that household.'

It was hot for May, thought Sandra as she prepared the food for the picnic. It should be perfect on the beach tonight. It would have been simpler to use more expensive cuts of meat for the barbecue, but the cost was prohibitive. The cheaper cuts would taste just as good in the end, but took more preparation. She prepared a marinade in which to put the tenderized steak and mixed mince and onion for hamburgers.

It was a pity the watermelon season was past. Slices of the bright red succulent fruit were always popular. She contented herself with making water ices of orange and lemon juice. Very refreshing and economical too. It must be wonderful to run a hotel like the Casa del Sol. Imagine having all that food to give people! I dare say we could feed our guests on what gets wasted there, she thought.

'What about your bathe?' asked Aunt Vi.

'I don't think I'll bother about it today. There's still lots to do.'

'Leave it now. You'll be working all evening. Perhaps you'll meet Craig,' said Aunt Vi hopefully.

'I hope not,' said Sandra.

She looked at Aunt Vi's bright eyes and thought, surely she doesn't think . . . how little she knows.

'I'm sorry to disappoint you, but from what little I've seen of him I just can't stand the man,' she informed her. 'He's brash and high-handed and loves his own way.'

'Now why have you taken such a dislike to the poor man?'

'Poor! That's the least of Craig's troubles. He's far too rich for his own good and seems to think money solves every problem.'

This afternoon she took care to take her wrap with her. She was determined not to suffer from the cold again today. But as yet it was beautifully warm. Goldie loped ahead of her, his golden pelt gleaming in the soft shimmering radiance of the winter sunlight. How she wished she had more time for the simple pleasures of the little seaside resort. It was so tempting to spend hours wandering along the shore, watching the sea-birds skimming over the water and the clear green turn of the waves.

In the height of summer the sand was often scorching hot to the foot at times and even the water was tepid and unrefreshing, as if, said Julie, one were bathing in warm soup. But now, in May, the autumn of the southern hemisphere, the weather was clear and beautiful, all humidity gone, and life could hold no greater pleasure than to run into the sparkling water, dive underneath the first foamy white breaker and emerge on the other side, then repeat the process until you found yourself in the stronger surf. Then it was a joy to catch a wave just before it broke and be propelled shoreward by its terrific force feeling like a dolphin, a sea creature not dependent upon two legs, but native to this strange element of tumbling water.

There was always the risk of getting tumbled over by an extra large breaker and after several beautiful glides in to the shore, Sandra found herself ignominiously flung down below the waves and emerged spluttering with eyes and mouth full of salt water and hair plastered across her face so that she could hardly see. She was swaying precariously, trying to regain her balance in the strength and fury of the following breaker, when she felt herself seized in strong arms.

'Need a little help, Sandra? I was lost in admiration at your expertise until this happened.'

Water-sodden and half-blinded by the spray as she was, Sandra had felt grateful to whoever was supporting her, but now she realized that it was Craig, she was not sure that she needed him.

'I'm quite used to this kind of thing,' she said, trying to be dignified but not succeeding very well in her half-drowned condition. 'Oh!' She was down again. Another wave had swamped her.

'We can't talk here. The waves are too strong,' said Craig, drawing her away and into more shallow water.

'Who wants to talk?' spluttered Sandra, but he did not appear to hear and went on guiding her inexorably towards the shore so that she felt like a small dinghy at the side of a sleek greyhound of a launch.

On the beach they found Kim in a peacock blue lurex swimsuit which had the effect of making her look sallow. Goldie had rolled over beside her and was lolling in the sand, his mouth drawn back in a foolish grin while he submitted to having his ears pulled. Kim looked absorbed and childlike as she played with the spaniel, but as soon as Craig and Sandra arrived she jumped up as if demanding their attention. Her expression was sulky as she demanded, 'She can bathe in the sea, so why can't I, Craig?'

'Sandra is obviously an expert swimmer. I'll take you in the sea when I'm satisfied you can swim properly.'

'I can swim, but I don't get enough practice because you're never at home and you won't let me swim alone,' Kim protested. She turned back to Goldie, suddenly forgetting her bad mood. 'This is a nice dog,' she said to Sandra. 'I wish I could have one.'

'Would you like to take him for a run along the beach?' asked Sandra. 'There's nothing he loves more.'

Away they ran, the golden dog with his curling plumes of ears streaming behind him and the slim girl who seemed again an eager child in spite of her precocious sophistication.

'We've never been settled anywhere before long enough to have a dog,' Craig explained. 'Never anywhere suitable, at any rate. Usually we've been in city hotels or apartments. I'm afraid Kim has led a very restless life with me.'

Sandra wondered what had happened to Kim's mother. She could not imagine that Craig would make any better a husband than he seemed to make a father. Kim was dreadfully spoilt. It was a pity, for basically there seemed to be something attractive about the child.

Craig glanced at the imposing house upon the ridge.

'I was determined to give her a home this time,' he said. Sandra smiled secretly. A home! That great bizarre mansion! Their small hotel with its collection of different buildings had been far more of a home, she was sure, than ever that house could be, despite its luxury.

She glanced up to find Craig regarding her quizzically.

'What are you considering so deeply?' he asked.

They were sitting on the sand and he idly poured sand upon her arm and then brushed it away.

'I was thinking,' she said, moving away slightly, 'that a house is not a home.'

He smiled mockingly and any temporary liking she was feeling for this hard-featured man vanished again.

'You'll be telling me next that money isn't everything!' he jibed.

'Nor is it, Mr. Ransom!' she said, springing to her feet and brushing away the sand his hands had left upon her. 'I'm sorry you appear to think I speak in clichés, but sometimes they can be true.'

Goldie came bounding back at that moment and Sandra felt herself free to go. How this man annoyed her with his presumption that wealth was all that mattered in the world!

'Let's go to the hotel swimming pool, Craig. It's boring on the beach,' said Kim.

Even his child preferred artificial amusements to the natural beauty of the sea and the shore. And no wonder when she had been brought up to Craig's ideas.

That evening the picnic on the beach just below Wave Crest was a great success. Quantities of hamburgers and steak rolls had been consumed and now the visitors had retired up to the lounge and were dancing merrily to the sound of recorded dance music.

After she had collected the remains of the picnic together, Sandra lingered on the beach enjoying the autumn night that was surprisingly mild, listening to the waves surging towards the shore and shining her torch on the crabs that scuttled around like shadowy ghosts of their more robust daytime selves.

She had thought she was alone on the beach, but in the distance she saw a tall slim figure coming towards her. He was walking along the edge of the surf, his head down, hands behind his back. And every now and again he kicked a pebble savagely as if this small action relieved some deep emotion. As he came nearer, she realized it was Gary. But if it were he, where then was Julie?

When he saw Sandra he seemed to swerve as if trying to avoid her, but then had second thoughts and approached her. His usual bright cheerful manner had deserted him and when he spoke she had a swift suspicion that he had been drinking more than was good for him.

'Hello, Sandra, nice to see you. I like to meet someone who enjoys the simple things of life.'

'Where's Julie?' asked Sandra.

'Where she wants to be, of course,' said Gary bitterly. 'In the Starlight Room of the Casa del Sol.'

'But how did she get there?'

'Like a fool I took her to have a drink beside the hotel pool after our swim this morning and she met the manager, Manoel de Villiers. She spoke to him about the interview on Monday and he asked her to dinner this evening. Of course she accepted. As she said to me, how could she refuse, when she's so keen to have the job? But all the same we had a flaming row, and here I am and there she is.'

Sandra put her arm on his sleeve.

'I'm so sorry, Gary. I'm sure it will come right. You know Julie.'

'I'm beginning to,' said Gary. He put his arm around Sandra and gave her a hug. 'But thanks for those kind words, anyway. You're a sweet thing, Sandra. I've always said so.' And he kissed her full on the lips.

She realized that although not drunk he had had more than he was usually accustomed to and while feeling sorry for himself was a little more amorous towards herself as if he wanted to prove that the hurt Julie had inflicted did not matter to him. She did not want to injure him more, so dared not protest, but withdrew quietly from his embrace.

'It's Julie you want, not me, Gary,' she told him, smiling. 'Why not go up to Aunt Vi and claim a cup of coffee? I know she has some on the stove.'

'Great idea, if you'll come with me, Sandra,' he said, and put his arm around her as they walked along the beach. Their path led them past a group of ski boats that were used for fishing, and as they drew near a figure who had been bending down over one of the boats straightened and shone the powerful light of a large torch upon them.

'Good evening, Sandra. It looks as if the beach picnic was a success.'

His dark face looked saturnine in the shadows behind the strong beam of light. It was Craig, but what did that matter? Why should she feel embarrassed that he had seen her with Gary's arm around her? It was nothing to him. He could draw what conclusions he wished to, if he was even interested.

CHAPTER THREE

'I HAD a fabulous evening,' Julie confided to Sandra when they met on Monday morning to present themselves for the interview. 'The Starlight Room is out of this world, silver fittings and grey velvet curtains and a dark blue ceiling covered with a replica of the sky. They even have clouds drifting past. You would think you were in the open air.'

'It must be dark to get that effect,' said Sandra.

'It is, my dear. I had to be quite severe with Manoel occasionally. But he's quite a dear and of course we had fabulous service, although because he's the manager he was called away every now and then, but he introduced me to some of his friends and we had quite a party. Mum was a bit fed up that I didn't get home until three a.m.'

'And what about Gary?' asked Sandra.

'He was a bit difficult, of course, but he'll come round. I'm longing to get work at the hotel and he should realize it's a wonderful opportunity. He should be glad I want to earn some money. He talks a lot of nonsense about getting married. I ask you ... on a reporter's salary! Why, he can't even afford to take me out anywhere special.'

'You shouldn't encourage him if he's serious and you're not,' reproved Sandra.

'Good grief, Sandra, you sound like a maiden aunt! Who would I go out with if I had to stop for everyone who got serious? They all want either marriage or an affair with me. I've had dozens of proposals one way or another, but marriage to a poor man is for the birds. Why, I can't even cook! But I'm sure there must be the right man for me somewhere, someone charming, fascinating, handsome, rich.'

'You don't need much, do you?' laughed Sandra.

Looking at Julie's lovely smiling face with its golden skin and emerald-bright eyes, she thought that cooking must be the last thing a man thought of when he was proposing to her. She was wearing a one-piece garment like a ballet dancer's practice dress, but it was white and showed her marvellous tan to perfection, clinging to the rather generous curves of her figure as if it had been sculptured upon her.

Sandra was wearing a brief pleated white skirt and navy sleeveless cotton sweater with a polo neck. She had brushed her dark gold hair on to her shoulders and tied it back with a navy ribbon, and she had applied a rose pink lipstick, but certainly she looked far less glamorous than Julie, who was wearing shimmering violet eye-shadow and sweeping artificial lashes below the lovely dark sweep of her cleverly shaped brows.

The entrance of the hotel was at road level and the building swept down in terraces towards the sea. There were green lawns with borders of bright pink pelargoniums and a large beautifully shaped swimming pool adorned with fountains and silver mermaids.

They were directed not to the Starlight Room which Julie had described but to a smaller room artificially illuminated even in the morning. In fact it might have been a theatre, so dim were the lights of the dance floor and the area surrounding this, where in the glimmer of

45

small wall lights one could see that the seats around the tables were in the form of benches made of glittering dark green leather material.

But the small stage was brilliantly lit up. It had been cleared of its recording apparatus and was evidently intended to play a part in the forthcoming interview. As Sandra and Julie became more accustomed to the light or lack of it, they realized that there were other girls waiting at the side of the stage. They were dressed in every variety of costume ranging through slacks, suits, brief shorts with see-through blouses, bikinis and elaborate evening dresses.

Sandra began to regret she had come. The close dark atmosphere oppressed her and she could imagine how noisy it would be when the volume of sound from all the recording apparatus was blasted into the small room. She had just decided to tell Julie she had changed her mind when there was a stir amongst the waiting girls, their lovely heads turned towards the door and Manoel, the manager, appeared.

Even in this dim light he looked a handsome man in a rather florid way, with glossy dark hair cut in Regency style, sleek moustache and small well-trimmed beard. He was wearing tight black slacks like those worn by a matador and his jacket was of ruby velvet with a frilled white shirt. To Sandra this seemed very strange garb for a morning in a beachside hotel, but Julie whispered, 'He's rather stunning, don't you think?' and the other girls surrounded him like a group of fluttering coloured butterflies.

He was accompanied by a young man whose sole duty appeared to be to agree with everything Manoel said, for at each remark he nodded his head. The twittering of the girls' voices was stilled as this young man raised his hands.

'Well, darlings,' said Manoel. He had a deep velvety voice and obviously knew how to make it sound charming.

'We won't have work for all you beautiful dollies, unfortunately, but we intend to take on about a dozen girls to dance with any of our patrons who need a partner and to act as hostesses in a general way. We would like you to be able to do a little go-go dancing too and we intend to provide uniforms . . . very glamorous outfits they are, I can tell you. Isn't that so, Keith?'

Keith nodded his head in agreement.

'Now we want you girls to walk up on to the stage one by one, and Keith and I can get some idea of what you look like and I'll ask you one or two questions just so we can get acquainted. How's that?'

There was a murmur of agreement from the girls. One girl, a little bolder than the rest, was heard to ask what the pay was and there were 'Ooh's' and 'Ah's' of pleased surprise when a generous sum was mentioned.

'I must try to get one of the jobs,' thought Sandra, changing her mind. 'It would be so well worth it even if it isn't exactly to my liking. We would be able to do so much with the extra money and it wouldn't take too much time.'

But when the interviews began, her determination began to waver as she realized what personal remarks Manoel thought himself entitled to make.

'Why need he be so frightfully rude?' she asked Julie, as a pretty girl dissolved into tears and hurried off the stage when he had imitated her broad South African accent. 'I've a good mind to go home.'

'Don't be like that, Sandra,' urged Julie. 'He has got to thin them out in some way. He'll probably think you sound too refined.'

'Nothing would surprise me,' said Sandra as another girl hurried away tearfully because he said her legs were like a prizefighter's.

Julie's turn came. She pirouetted up on to the stage, fully conscious of the lovely picture she made in the white clinging costume. The swinging black hair, the radiant smile, the bronzed beautiful legs, drew reluctant sighs of admiration from the other girls, and when she started to gyrate to the recorded music she looked a symbol of gaiety and joy of living.

'Lovely, darling,' said Manoel. 'I only wish we had a few more like you. Now, who's next? I hope we have another one who's a tired business man's dream. Sandra Hamilton. Let's have a look at you.'

Sandra knew she was at a disadvantage having to appear immediately after Julie. She walked rather reluctantly towards the stage. 'Come on, darling!' shouted the man called Keith. 'We haven't got all day, you know.'

Now she was in the full glare of the stage and could see only a few vague shapes in the black cave in front of her.

'Walk backwards and forwards across the stage. dear, will you?' asked Manoel.'H'm, h'm . . . yes . . . quite graceful, but not awfully sexy, I'm afraid, darling. Can't you put a bit more wiggle into it? Give it all you've got. The costume we're planning simply cries out for that.'

Sandra stood in the centre of the stage.

'I'm sorry,' she announced to the pit of blackness in front of her, 'I think I'm wasting your time and mine.'

A voice spoke up from the back of the room, somewhere amongst those shiny benches. It was a voice with a deep thrilling timbre, the one Gary had tried to imitate.

'Don't be quite so hasty, Miss Hamilton. Give Mr. de Villiers a chance to judge if you have the personality he needs.'

She could see the dim outline of a tall figure coming forward to join the other two men. There was a feminine flutter of excitement amongst the assembled girls as it was whispered around who the newcomer was.

Craig Ransom! Why hadn't she had her turn before he arrived? Or had he been here all the time and only now chosen to reveal his presence? She felt dreadfully selfconscious for a few moments and then a certain defiance she felt towards this man came to her aid. She walked some more, did a few dance steps and answered some rather simple questions in her low sweet voice.

There was a consultation between Manoel and Keith. Craig seemed to be standing aside, and declining to give an opinion. All that Sandra wanted was to walk away from the stage and out of this dark room into the brilliant light of the sunny winter's day. She tried to think of anything but the fact that she was standing in front of Craig at the mercy of his rather objectionable manager because she needed to earn money in some way.

Eventually Manoel turned towards her.

'So sorry, darling, we don't think you're altogether suitable. You're a bit too refined-looking and not enough curves in the right places, unfortunately. We need the girls to be a bit more sexy than you, though in a nice way, that goes without saying. Julie's the ideal type.'

She saw the glint of Craig's white teeth as he turned to Manoel and she realized he was smiling.

'I don't altogether agree with you there, Manoel, but of course it's for you to judge. I have seen Miss Hamilton in a bikini and I can tell you she has plenty of appeal when suitably dressed. Her costume is perhaps a little too restrained today. Charming, but it doesn't give the right impression.'

Sandra descended from the stage and approached Manoel and Craig.

'For your information, I really couldn't care less whether I give the right impression or not. You and your hotel have certainly failed to impress me. I'm only sorry that I've wasted my time and yours!'

Manoel glanced at her as if she was some rather distasteful kind of insect, but Craig, she noted angrily, was still smiling. Before he could say another word, however, she had found her way to the entrance and emerged on to the sunlit lawns.

She found her way around to the steps descending to the beach. It would do her good to walk home along the sea-front, she thought. The weather had changed and a south-westerly buster was whipping up the waves into white peaks of foam. But maybe a walk in this strong wind would help to soothe her ruffled spirits before she had to return to her hotel and her constant round of tasks.

If only she had found the atmosphere at the Casa del Sol congenial, and if only the manager had been less objectionable! Yet all the other girls seemed eager to have the job. Was it her own fault? Had she been too sensitive? Certainly now when she thought how useful the money would have been to them, she regretted her hastiness. What was it about Craig that aroused her hostility?

She was sure she could have tolerated Manoel and even fallen in with his wishes if it had not been that Craig was there. She had hated the way he told Manoel about her appearance in a swimsuit. How dared he discuss her in that manner with his manager! And yet if she had wanted the job, she should have been willing to put up with this, she knew. Well, it's too late now, she thought. But Aunt Vi is going to be disappointed even though she won't say much. It would have been an ideal way to earn extra money because normal kinds of jobs and ordinary working hours would take up too much of her time and she could not leave Aunt Vi to carry on alone. Now that it was too late, she wished she had been more tolerant.

In spite of the gathering wind there were a few people on the beach, for it was still sunny, but the sunbathers had retreated to sheltered places behind the rocks. Most of the bathers had come out of the water, for evidently they found the waves had become rough. She was surprised therefore when she saw a small figure in a bright costume walking into the sea, albeit a little hesitantly. After Craig's words the other day she was sure that Kim was not supposed to be bathing in the sea, especially in this wild weather, and as she drew near, she decided she had better interfere, however unpopular it was likely to make her.

'Kim,' she called, 'isn't the sea rather rough? Wouldn't it be better to bathe in the pool like you did yesterday?'

The little girl hesitated and Sandra thought for a moment she was going to ignore her, but she waded back into the shallow water almost as if she was glad of an excuse to postpone her swim. However, her reply was sulky enough.

'It's not very rough. Heaps of people have been swimming.'

'Have been, maybe. But you can see there are not many people going in now. If I were you I would wait until it's a bit calmer. Didn't I hear your father say you were not a very strong swimmer and were not allowed to go alone into the sea?'

Kim flashed a look of dislike at Sandra.

'Just because Craig said you were an expert swimmer it doesn't mean he thinks I'm no good.'

'Oh, Kim, you know I didn't mean that at all.'

What a difficult little girl Craig's daughter was, thought Sandra . . . like a small prickly hedgehog.

'I may not be as good as you, but I can show Craig I can swim in the sea. If I do it by myself today, tomorrow I can show him.'

She turned her back on Sandra and ran swiftly into the breakers that were pounding on to the beach. The tide was at an awkward phase and the waves were rushing up the shelving shoreline and falling back upon each other so that they formed a deep bubbling cauldron, quite close inshore. In a matter of seconds, Kim was out of her depth and being swept further out to sea. Sandra discarded her sandals and short skirt and plunged in after her.

She was not afraid, for she had been used to the sea for most of her life. She was only worried that she would not be able to reach Kim before she was swept even further away, for she knew that it would be a struggle to get ashore against the wayward currents of the receding tide. Fortunately the fact that the tide was going out helped her to swim swiftly and the bright yellow costume Kim was wearing helped her to locate her as she foundered helplessly in the strong waves.

'I can't get back,' Kim spluttered, yet Sandra was relieved to note that she did not appear to be very frightened. In fact she had not yet realized what a dangerous position she was in.

'I'll hold you and we'll swim back,' said Sandra. 'Don't hold on to me too tightly, otherwise it will be difficult to stay on the surface.'

She started back, but as she had surmised the return journey was more difficult and however strongly she swam she only seemed to gain a few yards and then would be swept back. At last, tiring somewhat, she started to tread water and encouraged Kim to do the same while still holding her.

How near the beach looked, and yet how far away! She wondered whether anyone had noticed their predicament. There was a seasonal shortage of lifeguards and during the winter there were no regular people doing this work. Suddenly above the noise of the sea she heard a shout.

'Try to stay where you are, Sandra, I'm coming!'

It was Craig, and in a short while he had appeared beside them and had taken command of the situation. Relieved of Kim's weight, Sandra was able to swim on her own to the shore and Craig with his extra strength was able to propel his daughter into shallow water.

They sank exhausted on to the sand and for a few moments could not even speak. Craig had discarded his safari jacket and was wearing a brief pair of shorts. Sandra's navy briefs and sleeveless top clung to her like a second skin. Her hair was dripping and she wrung it out, for she had nothing with which to attempt to dry it. Kim was the one who seemed least affected by the whole alarming episode.

'What on earth were you doing in the sea, Kim?' Craig asked.

Sandra noticed that his voice was mild and marvelled that a man of such determined character could be so gentle where his daughter was concerned.

'I wanted to practise so that I could go with you into the sea next time you bathed.'

Craig sounded remarkably patient with his difficult little daughter as he said, 'But I've told you that you must be able to swim properly before you go into the sea.'

'And when will that be? You never have time to teach me to swim properly. You're always saying you will, but you never do.'

Kim's face was sulky and her voice defiant, but Craig obviously thought this was no time to check her. The dangerous episode in the water was still too near to be angry with the child. He put his arm around her as if he were gentling a stubborn pony.

'Run up to the house now, there's my girl, and have a hot shower. I'll be there in a few minutes.'

'You promise faithfully?'

'Cross my heart.'

Kim strolled a shade reluctantly away from them. She seemed none the worse for her adventure. Sandra made to get up, but Craig stopped her.

'Just a minute, Sandra. Something has occurred to me.'

Sandra looked at the face of the dark man at her side. Julie would say he looked like a pirate now, she thought. His black hair was wet and curling, the dark

54

eyelashes spiky with moisture around his lively express-
ive grey eyes. He must spend a lot of time in the sun,
even though his work was concerned with that sophisticated hotel, for his broad shoulders and chest were
deeply tanned. His eyes met hers and he grinned suddenly.

'I've never seen anyone looking so wet. Your poor
hair! Do you know you have blue streaks all over your
face? No, don't rub it off. It looks like some kind of
make-up. Woad, maybe.'

Sandra realized that the navy ribbon with which she
had tied her hair must have lost its dye. Craig seemed
to regret that he had been tactless, for he put his arm
around her and held her shoulders in a firm grip.

'I want to tell you, Sandra, that I'm deeply grateful
for your help. I hate to think what might have happened if you hadn't been there at the right time.'

'It wasn't difficult,' Sandra disclaimed. 'Only a bit
exhausting. I've been used to swimming in all conditions since I was younger than Kim.'

'Yes, I realize you're an expert and that's exactly
what I want to speak to you about. Kim can swim in
the pool fairly well, but she doesn't seem very willing to
use it. I had thought when I had it installed that she
would use it a lot, under the supervision of one of the
servants, of course.'

'But it isn't much fun for a small girl to swim on her
own,' Sandra protested. 'At that age the beach is much
more interesting than a swimming pool, surely.'

'I don't see why you should think so.'

Sandra thought that if he couldn't see that the
beach with its golden sand, the sea of blue waves shot
with emerald green, the seagulls flying free over the
water, was much more delightful than any swimming

pool, then she could not attempt to explain it.

'She must learn to swim properly, and that's where you come in, I hope.'

'I?' asked Sandra. What now? she thought.

'I realized the other evening from your aunt's conversation that your hotel is going through a bad patch, and when I saw you at the interview this morning I realized that you were anxious to get a part-time job. I'm sorry about this morning. If it had been my choice . . .'

'Please don't talk about it. I realize I wasn't suitable for your requirements,' Sandra replied coldly. What a hypocrite the man was, pretending that he would have accepted her if it had not been for the manager!

'It has occurred to me that there's another job that I could offer you that would be very suitable, I hope. You could give Kim swimming lessons in the afternoons. Your aunt told me that you were usually free then.'

What has Aunt Vi been saying, and with what motive? thought Sandra.

'I would pay you well, naturally. It would be an individual post, so you would be paid better than the girls at the discothèque. Kim seems to have taken to you. I noticed that.'

I'd hate to be someone Kim hasn't taken to if Craig thinks that, thought Sandra. Why, the child looks at me most of the time as if she dislikes me intensely. But the money would be useful. And I'd be out in the open air too, not in that awful discothèque. But then it would mean I would lose the only time I really have to myself. But the money is more important than my leisure. I needn't even see Craig. He should be working at that time, surely. As for Kim, I've learned to cope with difficult guests at the hotel. Surely I can manage one small girl, however naughty.

'Very well, I'll do it,' she said.

'Good. You can start next week, I hope? That will give you a chance to get organized and for Kim to get used to the idea.'

CHAPTER FOUR

THE morning had been a particularly trying one for Sandra. Jabulani, the cook, although a faithful servant, was not particularly competent at the best of times, but Aunt Vi would never hear of any suggestions for a change of staff. Usually he confined his drinking to the week-ends, but last night he had been celebrating his son's coming of age and he was good for nothing today. Sandra had had to cook the breakfast for the visitors as well as carrying out the tasks of supervising the laundry and checking the supplies.

She would have liked nothing better than to relax on the beach and enjoy a refreshing swim, but this was the afternoon arranged for the first swimming lesson, so instead of bathing she had to face coping with Kim. Aunt Vi seemed to be the only one who was pleased at the turn of events.

'What did I tell you?' she demanded, her silver hair rising from her head like thistledown because she had just come from an expedition to cut the heads off the geraniums, the only flowers capable of flourishing in the window boxes facing the salt sea spray.

'As soon as I met Craig Ransom, I realized that he had not been sent to us merely by chance. It was meant to happen. I sensed as soon as I saw him that he was kind as well as charming and that he was destined to play an important part in our lives.'

'I wish you wouldn't be so enthusiastic about him, Aunt Vi, it's all perfectly simple. He has a daughter who needs to learn to swim. He knows that I can swim well. You mustn't imagine this personal interest in us. Craig Ransom is a man of the commercial world who knows when to seize on something that's to his own advantage. This is purely a business arrangement.'

She did not add, because she felt she had conveyed this to her aunt before, that she had an antipathy to Craig that made it difficult to accept favours from him even though she knew he would not do them if it did not benefit himself in some way.

Vi's blue eyes twinkled.

'Well, I for one believe in doing some positive thinking. He wouldn't do these things if he wasn't interested. It's quite plain to see he wants to know you better.'

Sandra was horrified at Vi's romantic notions, but she knew it would only hurt her aunt if she disclaimed them. Where Sandra was concerned she was like a hen with one chick, in spite of her sensible nature, and she thought every man who saw her must fall in love with her. Sandra, who had a practical notion of her own charms, was often embarrassed by this.

But she contented herself with saying mildly, 'I've only just met the man, and his charm evidently works more for you than me. In any case I don't expect to see him much. It's his daughter I'm going to teach, not him.'

Taking the short cut through the woods, so that Goldie, who accompanied her, could enjoy the walk, she could see the surf pounding on the beach below. But the lagoon at the end of the beach looked peaceful enough. That was one place that had been left beautiful. It had high rocky fern-covered cliffs on one side and a waterfall descending into the calm pool at its further end. The thought occurred to her that it would have been delightful to spend the afternoon swimming there. Perhaps when she had taught Kim to swim a bit better she could prepare her for swimming in the sea by first taking her to the lagoon.

She had arranged to meet Kim in the garden so that she did not need to go into the house, but when she arrived there was no sign of her. She spoke to one of the servants who promised to send a maid to look for Kim, and she herself made her way to the block of changing rooms with its sweeping façade that followed the lines of the pool, its white walls dripping with vivid red bougainvillea, with here and there an Ali Baba jar filled with shining dark green exotic plants.

When she came out of the changing room there was still no sign of her prospective pupil, but she could hear Goldie barking frantically. This was most unusual, for he was normally a quiet dog. The pool was surrounded by coloured terrazzo tiles and there were gaily striped umbrellas and low lounging seats with bright cushions. She was rather surprised to hear a splashing noise from the further and deeper end of the pool, although she was too far away to see who the occupant was.

But of course it must be Kim, and she felt disturbed that the child had ventured in without her and at the deep end too. This must be more bravado. Kim must be determined to show her she could swim without her help.

But when she arrived at the side of the pool, she had a nasty shock. The occupant was a large leguan, a monitor lizard that looked like some prehistoric monster. It was about five feet long and was swimming around looking for some way to get out, threshing its tail and hissing fiercely, obviously in a very bad temper at its predicament and now even more agitated by Goldie's barking. While Sandra stood astonished by this sight and wondering what to do, she heard a loud giggle coming from behind the low wall surrounding the pool. Undoubtedly the appearance of the monster was some of Kim's contriving.

'Kim, come here!' she called.

Kim sidled out looking rather sheepish but at the same time pleased with herself. She had not changed into a bathing suit but was wearing a rather elaborate pair of slacks with Tyrolean embroidery.

'Hello, Kim, I've come to give you a swimming lesson. Had you forgotten about it?' asked Sandra pleasantly.

Kim shrugged her shoulders.

'We can't swim with that in the pool, can we? Besides, I don't want swimming lessons from you. Craig must teach me.'

So that was the reason for the rebellion. She wanted more attention from Craig.

'Your father doesn't have much time. Obviously he's a busy man. Why not let me teach you and then later when you know how to swim properly you can be with Craig when he goes into the sea.'

Kim's grey eyes regarded Sandra with critical appraisal, but Sandra gazed directly back at her. What had she expected? – that she would scream and run at sight of the leguan? And if it was Kim's trick, as it was, of course, how on earth had she got the creature into the pool? It had made the water so dirty with its struggles, not to mention the mud it had brought into the pool, that it certainly would not be possible to give Kim a swimming lesson here today – but what was she to do? Sandra hated to admit defeat on the first occasion she was to take up this job.

'You'd better call one of the gardeners to catch this

poor creature and release it in the bush.'

'I'll call Jacob. He put it in.'

'On your instructions, I suppose. Really, Kim, that was a foolish thing to do.'

Kim looked slightly ashamed. 'I thought it would be a funny trick.'

And you didn't want a swimming lesson from me, thought Sandra.

Aloud, she said, 'Well, now we have no alternative but to use the hotel swimming pool.'

Kim looked somewhat taken aback.

'Oh, please don't let's go there. Craig may be there and then he'll find out what I did. I suppose you'll tell him just as soon as you see him, won't you?'

'No, I won't, Kim. If you really don't want to go to the hotel pool, I have another idea. We can swim in the lagoon. It's quite safe and fairly shallow. Just for once it will do instead of the pool.'

Kim seemed relieved that Sandra had promised not to tell Craig about her prank, so they left two gardeners fishing out the angry leguan and headed for the beach. As Sandra had thought, the lagoon was delightful for swimming this afternoon. It depended very much on the condition of the tide whether it was deep enough, and today it was just right for a beginner.

With the aid of a board, Sandra started to teach Kim to hold herself in the water and do the correct leg movements, for she had noticed she was inclined to do a dog paddle of her own invention. At last she seemed to be making some headway with the rebellious little girl. Kim became absorbed in the lesson and Sandra reflected that as long as she was the centre of interest Kim was happy. In fact she had been so diligent that Sandra allowed a little licence when the lesson was over and they started imitating ducks with much laughter while Goldie barked frantically from the sandbank.

All at once Sandra was aware of a tall figure standing on the shore. 'Oh, look, there's Craig!' shouted Kim, but as they approached him he did not respond very heartily to his daughter's delighted greeting, for his face was frowning and he looked altogether displeased.

'I thought it was understood, Sandra, that you should teach Kim in the pool. What's the use of owning one if you bring her to this place which I'm sure can't be very hygienic?'

Sandra was somewhat at a loss. Kim cast an imploring glance at her and she remembered that she had promised that Craig should not know about the trick with the leguan.

'Be a dear and go to fetch Goldie for me,' she asked Kim. 'It was such a lovely day and the lagoon looked so perfect for bathing we decided to come down here,' she said rather weakly. 'It's a tidal pool and the water from the sea comes in every day. I'm sure it's almost as clean as a swimming pool.'

Cleaner than yours was a while ago, she thought.

'I would have preferred that Kim swam in the pool, nevertheless. She's an active little girl and you might have had trouble in keeping her in order in these surroundings. There's always the danger of her getting out of her depth.'

'You may be sure, Mr. Ransom, that I took every care of her. But this won't happen again. If you want her to swim in the pool, she will in future.'

'I can't understand why you brought her here today. Please understand, Sandra, that I'm not prepared to pay you for playing around in the lagoon. I think it would be best if we call it all off. It's pretty obvious that you're a self-willed young woman not prepared to fall in with anyone else's wishes.'

Saying that he had urgent business to attend to at the hotel, he strode away abruptly, leaving Sandra feeling very snubbed.

'Where's Craig?' demanded Kim, when she returned from running along the beach with Goldie. 'I thought he would stay to see how my swimming was going.'

She looked disappointed.

'No, he had to go.'

'Was he mad that you'd brought me here?'

'Yes, he was.' There was no sense in mincing matters with Kim. 'In fact he doesn't want me to continue with the lessons.'

'Oh, but. . . .'

'That's what you wanted, isn't it, Kim?'

'Yes, I did at first, but now I want to go on learning to swim. This lesson was fun.'

'You should have thought of that before.'

Sandra was sorry that the swimming lesson had turned out to be such a fiasco. In spite of her naughtiness, there was something appealing about Kim and Sandra felt she could have got on with her if only Craig had not arrived upon the scene. However, if he had decided she was not to be trusted to look after his precious child, there was little she could do.

It was fortunate that when Sandra returned to the hotel some new visitors had arrived and Aunt Vi was busy showing them around the place. She felt sad at this turn of events and hated to feel the new venture had failed so soon. On top of this she felt quite bruised by Craig's attitude. It was true he was very sensitive about Kim's welfare, but how could he have thought it was wrong to take her to the lagoon? Of course he did not know about Kim's trick with the leguan. But all the same she felt he had been very hasty. In fact he had lived up to her first impression of him. He had said himself that he was a dangerous man to cross.

Well, it could not be helped, but all the same she felt an almost physical hurt at his unkindness. How foolish! Why should she feel like this? She had led a far from sheltered life. In the hotel trade there were inevitably people who were difficult or unpleasant and she had learned to accept this and to deal tactfully with them. So why should she feel so sensitive with regard to Craig Ransom?

She had showered and changed and had just been to see that Jabulani had everything he needed for the hotel dinner when a small bright yellow sports car drew up in the hotel grounds with a great roaring of its engine and Julie stepped out, her dark hair swinging. She was dressed in purple velvet shorts, a cream satin blouse and high cream-coloured boots.

'Hi, Sandra,' she called. 'It seems ages since we met. So much has happened.'

'What a smart car. Whose is it?' asked Sandra, for she thought she would have heard about it if Julie had acquired one of her own.

'I borrowed it from a dream of a young man at the Casa del Sol. I told him I wanted it for just half an hour. I simply had to come to see you. Sandra, I've met him!'

'Who?' asked Sandra, but she thought at once that she knew who Julie meant.

'Craig Ransom. Oh, Sandra, he's the most gorgeous man I've ever met!'

Sandra smiled a little crookedly.

'I seem to have heard that before, Julie.'

'I know, pet, but this time I really mean it. Can't we sit for a minute? I must tell you all about him.'

They made their way to a white seat on the lawn high above the ocean. The sun had almost gone and the dark sea was the colour of a ripe plum beneath the rosy clouds.

'He asked to be introduced to me the very first night I worked at the hotel and he danced with me three times and said the most flattering things about my dancing and how I looked. Oh, Sandra, this time it's real, I know it. I've never felt like this before. He's the most wonderful man I've ever met.'

'Have you ... did he ask you to meet him again?' asked Sandra.

'That's another thing I wanted to tell you. He didn't exactly ask me, but he said did I know of a quiet place up the coast where it would be good to dine. I'm sure he's going to ask me and I told him about the Sea Urchin. I must get a new dress. Come to Mum's boutique tomorrow and help me choose it. I must fly now, but I had to tell you all about it.'

'Aren't you going to see Gary while you're here?'

'Gary? No, I think not. The less I see of him the better at the moment. He acts so awkwardly when we meet. Anyone would think we'd been engaged, and there was never anything of the kind between us. You know that very well, don't you, Sandra?'

With a gay wave of her hand she was off. The car made a singing noise all the way down the drive and sounded very impressive. Just when it had disappeared, Gary came out of his rondavel yawning.

'Who was that? I was just having a nice kip when it

66

woke me. I had to catch up on some sleep because I was out on a story until all hours last night.'

'It was Julie. She told me not to disturb you.'

This was partly true, thought Sandra.

'You can't bluff me, Sandra. She isn't very interested in seeing me these days. She has bigger fish to fry.'

Sandra hardly felt she could deny this.

'Getting that hotel job has given Julie large ideas. She sees too much glamour and luxury there to be contented with an evening at the drive-in and hamburgers and coffee any more. If only I could catch the editor's eye with some big scoop instead of having to hand out all these dreary reports of village talk as "our local correspondent".'

Sandra could not help feeling sorry for Gary, although she did not really think he had a chance with Julie. Everything was against him, the fact that Julie's mother was keen for her to marry someone rich and now the fact that she had met Craig.

'I've often thought,' she said, 'that the arrival of the fishing boats on to the beach at early light would make a good feature for the newspaper. What do you think?'

She had diverted his thoughts, which was what she had wanted to do.

'Yes, it's an idea, certainly. Not world-shaking, but it might earn me a bit extra. Do they come in every morning?'

'Most mornings unless the weather is too rough. I'm going down to the beach to meet them tomorrow to try to get some fish for the kitchen. Would you like to come?'

'Yes, I'll come. You're quite a bright girl, Sandra.

How about getting me an interview with your friend Craig Ransom? I'd give a lot to be able to do a feature on his house. He's refused every newspaperman who's approached him so far.'

Sandra shook her head. 'I'm afraid that isn't possible. He's not my friend, incidentally.'

In fact he looks like becoming my enemy, she thought.

Next morning at five-thirty, while on this winter's morning it was still dark, Sandra pulled on some slacks and a thick cream-coloured sweater with an Aran pattern that Vi had knitted for a birthday present some years ago. There was a faint streak of pink cloud on the horizon and a glimmer of grey light was making the outlines of trees and bushes just discernible.

Jabulani had not yet lit the coal stove, so she brewed coffee on a Primus and took it to Gary's hut. He had already dressed and was gathering together his photographic equipment.

It was chilly on the beach and the sands looked a uniform grey backed by the dark sea with its cold-looking white-topped breakers. Several Indians were fishing already. They came to fish before going to work, for they usually had large families to feed and little money to spare. Not one fish was thrown back, for however small it would be useful in the large curry pot.

Goldie had come with them and ran tirelessly up and down the beach after the small sea-birds gathering in the dawn along the water's edge. The sudden sharp bark that he gave when he became unbearably excited, the swish of the waves and the occasional whiplike song of a fishing rod being cast out into the sea were the only sounds besides the lonely calls of the sea-birds winging their way across the water and occasionally plummeting like stones in their endless search for food.

'When are these boats going to arrive?' asked Gary. The end of his sharp nose was pink and he stamped his feet for warmth. Sandra produced the coffee and sandwiches and they tramped up and down the beach feeling a little better. Gary had brought fieldglasses and scanned the dark ocean impatiently whenever they paused, and at last he was rewarded. 'Look!' he shouted, and at the same time the Indian fishermen started calling to each other and pointing out to sea.

At first only a darker shape could be seen upon the water coming swiftly towards the beach. Then as the boat reached the breakers one or two Indians downed their rods and went to fetch the trailers that were placed high above the tidemark. The ski boat was long and powerful, tilted at one end and small at the other. It slewed around in the shallow water and several men jumped out waist-deep. They were wearing rubber wet suits such as are worn by skin divers and Gary rushed forward to take photographs, but Sandra waited until they had come in, then she approached the skipper of the boat, a rugged-looking man with a beard. He was just opening the deep compartment that held the catch.

'It looks as if the fishing was good last night,' she commented, for it was full of grunter.

'Not bad,' the man replied.

'I hope you'll be able to let me have some today, Jake.'

'I'm afraid not, Miss Hamilton. I have to supply the hotel's order and there won't be any left after that.'

'Surely you can spare a few for us, Jake? We don't need many, but our visitors expect fish when they come to a seaside place.'

Jake looked uncomfortable at having to refuse Sandra.

'I'm sorry, Miss Hamilton. Much as I'd like to I can't afford to short supply the hotel. I make a lot out of them, you know, during the season.'

Sandra turned aside to Gary who had paused to change his lens.

'Always the hotel,' she sighed. 'They used to beg us to buy fish before, and now we can never get any.'

The dark silhouette of another boat could be seen approaching in the blinding first rays of the sun that was making the water throw off glittering sparks as if a million sardines were leaping in the ocean. Gary was still taking photographs and Sandra turned to watch the boat approach, hoping that maybe this one's skipper had fish to spare.

The figures of the men were black in their clinging rubber wet suits against the shining light of dawn. They looked like beings from another planet. She noticed one taller than the rest. He was laughing and joking with the others, but then he leapt from the boat into the waist-deep water and started wading out, striding strongly against the heavy swell. The rays of sunlight gilded the wet drops on his dark hair and made his tanned face ruddy, and she realized it was Craig.

She turned aside, not wanting to have to greet him after yesterday's scene, but to her surprise he came directly towards her, smiling in so irresistible a way that she felt her taut emotions relaxing and found herself smiling back.

'You're certainly an early riser, Sandra. I was going to phone you to ask if I could see you today.'

She wanted to say that this was certainly a sudden change from yesterday, but confronted by that smile and the dancing eyes that were the colour of the silver-flecked sea the words died on her lips. He was apparently just going to explain his statement when Gary approached, camera in hand. Of course he wants an introduction, thought Sandra. He's keen to get an interview. But she obstinately remained quiet. There was an awkward silence and the two men glanced rather warily at each other like antelope skirmishing for a fight, and Sandra, weakening in her determination, changed her mind and introduced them since Craig, she thought, could defend himself quite adequately against the power of the press.

'I've hoped to meet you for a long time,' Gary informed Craig. 'I got what I hope will be a very good shot of you and the ski boat. Do you mind if I give your name when it's published? It adds interest if I can mention a well-known public figure in an article.'

'I suppose there can be no objection to that,' Craig replied a little grudgingly. 'It hasn't anything to do with the hotel. I went out just for the fun of it. But let me see it beforehand, there's a good chap.'

This was just the opportunity Gary had been waiting for, Sandra knew, for he had told her already that he was very eager to see the house.

'I'll deliver it at your home personally,' he promised, and Sandra wanted to smile when Craig said, 'Don't do that. You'll always find me at the hotel in the mornings and evenings. I don't like to be disturbed at the house.'

'People are very interested in your home, Mr. Ransom,' Gary persisted. 'How about an interview with pictures of your house and your young daughter?'

Sandra saw Craig freeze up. The genial manner which had surprised her vanished and the man whose grim looks had given her her first bad impression returned.

'I don't give interviews in a private capacity, young man. Naturally I welcome publicity for the hotel, but my private life is my own and I like to keep it so. And another thing – I don't intend that every Tom, Dick and Harry of a newspaper reporter should feel free to interview my young daughter. I want no publicity for her.'

He turned to Sandra.

'I'd be glad if you could come to see me at the house if you can spare any time this afternoon. There are some things that need to be cleared up and I can't deal with them except in private.'

This seemed a snub for Gary, and Sandra again felt indignant at Craig's high-handed methods.

'I don't know of anything that has to be cleared up between us, Mr. Ransom,' she said. 'I thought we'd completed all our business yesterday.'

'I don't think so. I would be very glad to see you some time during the day. I'll phone you later.'

What he had to say was definitely not for Gary's ears, it seemed.

At this moment Jake approached Craig and whispered to him, 'Miss Hamilton was wanting some fish for their hotel, sir, but I told her you would be needing all the catch, but since I saw you talking to her so friendly I wondered whether. . . .'

Sandra cut into his suggestion abruptly.

'We can do without the fish. I wouldn't dream of depriving your visitors, Mr. Ransom.'

'Of course you must have some. Don't be a silly girl.

I never knew you were being refused it, Sandra. Take as much as you need.'

How terrible! Now she had to feel patronized by Craig again. And yet what could she do? It would seem crazy to refuse now in front of Gary and Jake.

As they walked back along the beach with an Indian helping them to carry their load of fish, Gary commented, 'Quite a guy, this pal of yours, isn't he?'

'I'm sorry he was so rude to you when you asked him about the house.'

'Think nothing of it, pet. We newspapermen are a tough lot. I'll get that interview one of these days, just you wait and see.'

Sandra wondered what Craig intended to say when he phoned her. Doubtless she would soon find out.

CHAPTER FIVE

LATER when Sandra came out of the kitchen after giving Jabulani his instructions for the day, she was surprised to see a small figure helping Aunt Vi to feed and water the birds and animals. Kim seemed to be chattering to her as if she had known her all her life, but Vi did seem to have that effect on people. However, when Sandra came towards them she was silent.

'Kim has come to tell you something,' said Vi, brushing aside the blue crane which had its head in the seed packet trying to get more than its fair share. Kim's eyes, so wide and grey, had an anxious expression.

'I came to tell you I'm sorry about yesterday, Sandra. I told Craig what I'd done and he said if I said sorry perhaps you might come back to teach me, but you didn't have to, of course, if you didn't want to.'

So this accounted for Craig's change of attitude.

'Of course I accept your apology Kim, but the important point is what do you really want? Do you want me to teach you to swim? You didn't seem to be very keen yesterday. Certainly not at first.'

Kim looked at her imploringly.

'I want you to come back. I liked our lesson. I'm sorry about the leguan. It was a dumb thing to do, I guess.'

'And the poor wee creature can't have enjoyed its swim much, either,' added Vi.

'It wasn't very little,' said Kim, a small giggle escaping. 'It was enormous, wasn't it, Sandra?'

'It certainly was,' Sandra agreed.

Sandra was glad that Kim had plucked up courage to come to see her on her own and to apologize, even though it seemed to have been at Craig's instigation. At least she had been honest about her trick. On the other hand she thought it was in keeping with Craig's arrogant nature that he had sent Kim but did not appear to think it necessary to apologize himself. After all, he had been very brusque and rude to her yesterday and knew now that she had really not been at fault.

The promised phone call had not been forthcoming. She supposed Kim's visit was in lieu of this. However, it was hardly the child's fault that she had a father like Craig and she would go to give her a lesson this afternoon, hoping that she need not see him.

She wore her white pleated skirt with a primrose knitted sweater today and her honey-coloured gold-streaked hair was brushed back severely, for she knew she would probably get it wet during the lesson. The swimming pool had been cleaned and was crystal clear. It was no wonder really that Craig preferred that Kim should swim here, for it seemed so luxurious with its mosaic design of tritons and mermaids in cool shades of green and aquamarine.

This afternoon Sandra was almost sorry Craig did not put in an appearance since the swimming lesson went so well and, even in this short time, Kim seemed to show signs of improvement. But there was no sign of him. Evidently he had decided to let her get over the resumption of the lessons without his presence, though she could not imagine he would feel embarrassed by the memory of his own ill temper.

Having said goodbye to Kim, Sandra was making her way towards the imposing natural wood gate that led out to the woodland road. It was good that Kim had become friendly and amenable, yet for some reason Sandra felt strangely flat and depressed. She was mystified as to why she should feel like this, because surely now she should feel more cheerful after the conflicting emotions she had experienced yesterday. And on the practical side it was good to feel that after all she was able to earn some money to help with the problems of the hotel.

Her thoughts were interrupted by the sound of footsteps upon the gravel of the driveway. Then someone grasped her shoulders and swung her around to face him. It was Craig, hardly recognizable as the frowning man of the day before, smiling down at her with a glint of wickedness in the dark grey eyes, the unruly lock of hair falling forward as he leaned towards her.

'Sandra! I'm glad I caught you. Have you time to talk to me for a few moments? Or are you rushing off to do some more organizing?'

In view of her previous thoughts, Sandra was surprised to hear herself saying that Aunt Vi could cope for a while and to find herself being drawn in to the house and accepting an offer of coffee. She had to admit that Craig had a way with him when he chose to be charming. He apologized very sincerely for his mistake of yesterday.

'It was a bit naughty of Kim, but now she seems quite happy about the lessons,' said Sandra.

'She's a monkey,' Craig said, not sounding too perturbed about it. 'But I wouldn't have her otherwise. I like a child with spirit. She'll certainly need it to cope with life at the pace we live it these days.'

As you live it, Sandra amended silently. Looking up, she found that Craig was gazing at her very attentively, as if trying to read her thoughts.

'You haven't said yet whether you've forgiven me,' he commented.

She found it very difficult to meet that direct grey gaze.

'Haven't I shown that by coming back to teach Kim?' she asked.

'Ah, but that's for Kim's sake, not mine.'

She had turned her head, ostensibly to watch through the window a flock of sea-birds wheeling in flight above the dark blue water, and had not heard any movement, but suddenly he was beside her holding her chin in his hand and turning her face towards him.

'Look at me and tell me I'm forgiven.'

She could not draw herself away, but her eyes closed, for she was reluctant to surrender to the confused clamour of her senses that arose from his nearness and the firm touch of his hand.

'Of course,' she said, striving to keep her voice level.

'Open your eyes and say, "Craig, you're forgiven".'

When she did so, his expression was compelling, but above the firm set of the mouth his eyes had the tenderness she had formerly thought was reserved for Kim. Like a child at school she repeated his words and he released her, laughing.

'And to show you've truly pardoned me, you must put up with my company for a whole evening. I believe there's a very good little place called the Sea Urchin along the coast where one can dine and dance. How about it, Sandra? Will you come with me next Wednesday evening?'

This was the place Julie had mentioned, and with the thought of Julie, Sandra struggled to regain her common sense. It would be madness to accept the invitation. It would mean nothing to Craig, just another evening with a girl to fulfil an obligation.

'I'm usually far too busy to go out during the week. There's really no need for you to invite me to dinner, Craig. Let's forget about the whole of yesterday. I don't need any compensation.'

For all the notice he took of this she might as well not have spoken.

'That's a date, then, Sandra. Expect me at six.'

'No,' said Sandra firmly, 'I really mean it. I can't come with you, Craig.'

'What a difficult girl you are! But I told you when we first met that I don't take no for an answer.'

'This time you'll have to.'

She rose to go, but it seemed she was not to lose his company so easily.

'Oh, don't go yet. Let me show you around my house, Sandra. You see how hard I'm trying to please you. You'll be my first guest to see it properly. I want to keep this side of my life, my home life with Kim, private. Newspaper and magazine editors have been pestering me to let them write articles about it, but I'm not keen they should do so. They can write as much as they like about the hotel, naturally. I'm all for publicity where my business is concerned, but I want this house to be Kim's home, not just a showplace.'

They had been sitting in a small sitting room, more intimate than the large drawing room which Sandra had seen on her previous visit, for it was furnished in a modern way with white-framed chairs cushioned in deep orange and a shaggy deep cream carpet. With its brightly patterned curtains and magazine rack and record player there was a more homely atmosphere than Sandra would have believed possible in this huge house.

But now Craig led the way to the other rooms, to Kim's suite where there was deep rose-coloured carpeting, a pink bathroom, frilly curtains and a separate dressing room with a wall of cupboards to hold Kim's clothes.

Craig's study, at the top of the house up a narrow staircase, had casement windows that looked far over the sea. There was a small telescope and Sandra noticed that a pair of binoculars lay on the tooled leather-topped desk.

But it was in the main bedroom that the interior decorators seemed to have let their ideas run riot. The huge louvred windows across the wall facing the sea were festooned with heavy looped curtains from floor to ceiling in a spectacular design of turquoise and purple. The bedhead fastened to the wall behind the huge bed was quilted in turquoise velvet and the fitted carpet was of violet.

'How do you like it?' asked Craig.

'It's very impressive,' said Sandra. 'I've never seen anything like it before.'

It was impressive, certainly, with the wide view of the ocean setting off the beautiful proportions of the room and its furniture, but there was nothing personal about it at all. It could have been some show house invented by architects and decorators. What kind of a man was Craig, she wondered, that he depended upon other people to make his home for him and did not let any glimmer of his own personality show? Or was this his personality? Did he believe in showing this façade of wealth to the world, requiring all this luxury to create the image of a wealthy man?

He was showing her the dressing room now, a place of sliding doors that revealed every variety of tailored suit, jacket and so on. And here upon a small table she saw the first sign of anything connected with Craig's past. It was a photograph, and not a very good one, obviously taken by some back street photographer and printed on cheap paper which had yellowed with age. But the face that looked out at Sandra was delicate and sweet, the dark hair parted in the middle, the huge eyes a little sad, the hands clasped in a pose that suggested that of a dancer.

Craig must have noticed her interest in the photograph, but he did not respond and she felt unable to ask about it. He turned away abruptly and led her back into the main bedroom where they paused at the window overlooking the sea. From here could be seen the vast cliff of the Casa del Sol and the chalets and swimming baths connected with Craig's enterprises.

'I sometimes pinch myself and wonder if I'm dreaming,' Craig said slowly. 'I think that some day I'll wake up and find this all vanished and that I'm back in the little room where my life began.'

'And where was that?' asked Sandra.

His grey eyes had lost their hardness and had a brooding look, but he spoke as if the words were forced out of him.

'In the back street of a grey north-country industrial town where we went hungry most of the time. But you aren't interested in my past ... or present, for that matter. In that respect you're unlike most women I meet, who are distinctly interested in my present life so long as it's prosperous.'

Sandra was silent. But her curiosity was aroused. She had assumed that Craig had always been a rich man. His careless arrogance seemed to bear this out. Certainly she had never thought that he had known poverty or hunger. But now it seemed she was wrong. She glanced through the open door in the direction of the photograph and he followed her gaze. His mouth was bitter now.

'Yes, the girl in the photograph was my wife, Kim's mother. She died when Kim was very young, just before the tide of luck turned and I began to do well in business. We were very poor, but because she believed in me she wouldn't let me take a nine-to-five clerk's job but encouraged me to follow my own ambitions. We eked out a living on my poor earnings supplemented by her wage from dancing in a cheap cabaret. It was always bitterly cold coming home at night and we had no transport. She developed pneumonia and died before our hopes were fulfilled.'

'I'm so sorry,' Sandra said.

'Strange. I haven't spoken of her for years. No one here knows the story. Certainly not Kim.'

He took Sandra by the shoulders and looked at her intensely, and this time she could not turn away. The grey eyes were no longer steely but soft as the mist that even now was creeping in from the sea below the house.

'There's something gentle about you, Sandra, something different from the usual women I meet, in spite of your ability to run the hotel which I can understand is tough going. I was hasty yesterday, but Kim is very precious to me, as you must realize. Don't disapprove of me too much, will you? Kim likes you and would be so pleased if we could be friends.'

81

He leaned forward and kissed her gently on the brow, smiling in so charming a way that it would have been impossible to draw away.

Later she refused his offer of a lift and walked home alone. She wanted to sort out the strange mixture of feelings that seemed imperceptibly to have invaded her heart, for she knew she could not feel enmity to him any more however arrogant he might appear to the world at large. And yet she was afraid now that some of the antagonism she felt for Craig had gone, afraid to examine too closely the feeling that had welled up in her as he held her to him and gently looked down into her eyes.

CHAPTER SIX

SOME days had passed and Sandra had settled down into the usual routine of keeping the hotel. Several times she had gone to give Kim her lesson, but she had not seen Craig again nor was she sure that she wanted to. He had not phoned to renew his request that she should go out to dinner with him as he had said he would. She was quite sure in her heart that he had not really meant it when he had said he would not accept her refusal. Someone as busy as he was could not be expected to renew invitations that had been refused once.

Nevertheless when the day came that would have been the one on which she might have had a dinner date with Craig she felt a little forlorn, for it would have been fun to accept and find herself whisked away to that small restaurant along the coast and to have spent the evening in Craig's company, however little the date would have meant to him. However, it was her own fault. She had had the opportunity to accept and she had chosen to refuse. So what did it matter? She had many more important things to think about. Things such as Aunt Vi's sudden determination to make marmalade.

Vi had come to her this morning, her hair standing out in a silver aureole around her head as it did when she was particularly excited and had been running her fingers through it as she pondered over some plan.

'I've had a grand idea, Sandra. Do you recall that this week we got a lot of low-priced grapefruit and oranges on the market? We'll never be able to use them all for breakfast. So I propose I should make marmalade out of them. That way we'll kill two birds with one stone. We'll use up the fruit and we'll save on not having to buy preserves for a while.'

'But won't it be an awful lot of work for you, Aunt Vi?'

Vi's blue eyes twinkled.

'I'll get Jabulani to help cut the fruit and I'll use the old pressure cooker so as not to waste fuel.'

'But we haven't used the pressure cooker for ages because it wasn't very satisfactory last time we tried it.'

'Oh, there's nothing really wrong with it. Wait and see. You get finer marmalade when it's made in a pressure cooker. It will be clearer and a better colour.'

'I hope you're right,' Sandra said doubtfully.

Aunt Vi set about her task with great enthusiasm. It took herself and Jabulani a couple of hours to chop up the fruit and then she had to make the syrup, but by late afternoon she had it in the pressure cooker, which was a large hotel type utensil though rather an antique. Sandra offered to stay in to supervise the cooking, but Vi was determined that she should not miss her swim because this afternoon Kim was going into town with a friend and had to miss her lesson.

It was so pleasant having a swim in the sea without having to be responsible for a lesson. She had forgotten how much she enjoyed plunging into the water and surfing in on the breakers. As she was drying herself and preparing to go back, Julie arrived and, dismissing her escort, asked Sandra to take a stroll along the beach.

'I'm so glad I met you, Sandra. I have wonderful

news. Manoel has asked if Mum and I would like to go with him and Craig when they travel up the coast one weekend to inspect some land they hope to buy.'

Sandra found she experienced a physical pang of dismay. This was terrible! She should be pleased for Julie's sake that she had found someone of whom her mother could approve, someone who seemed eminently suitable for Julie's sophisticated nature. What hope had she herself of ever raising Craig's interest? And even if she did, their temperaments were completely opposed. No, Julie with her beauty and gay disposition was much more suitable for Craig.

'I'm sure that even though it was Manoel who proposed we should go the suggestion really came from Craig. And oh, Sandra, I'm so thrilled! Mum likes him too. Everything seems to be going so well. I'm sure he only has to meet me more often to begin to have ideas of marriage. He would never have proposed this jaunt up the coast if he hadn't been really interested in me. And the fact that he asked Mother too shows that he's serious about it, don't you think?'

Sandra agreed that this was so.

As she wandered slowly back to the hotel she wondered why this conversation had made her feel so depressed. She knew very well that she could never hope to interest Craig and with all the upsets she had had with him she doubted whether she wanted to. Nevertheless she could not feel wholeheartedly pleased that Julie seemed to have attracted him.

She was wrenched away from thoughts of romance as soon as she arrived back at the hotel by the sight of Jabulani running out from the kitchen as if Tokoloshe, the mischievous African sprite, was after him. When he saw Sandra, he ran towards her and began to stammer,

'Oh, Miss Sandra, come quick! The pressure cooker he go "Vroom, vroom" and then he start to whizz round. I not know how to stop him.'

Sandra hastened to the kitchen and was confronted with the sight of the cooker's top whirling around to let off steam and spraying jets of hot marmalade over the whole of the kitchen both upon the ceiling and upon the walls.

There was nothing to be done until the cascade had slowed down and then Sandra managed to grasp the pot in both hands and take it outside. Returning to inspect the damage, she found that everywhere she looked there were sticky trails. It was amazing how far a pot full of marmalade could go in covering a whole room.

While she and Jabulani were making a start at cleaning up the mess, Vi returned. Having put the marmalade to cook, she had gone off to feed the birds and had straightaway forgotten all about it.

An hour later, Sandra herself felt hot and sticky, but the kitchen was restored to some kind of order, and she reflected fleetingly that it was just as well she had not taken Craig's invitation seriously, for she could never have been ready in time.

Just then she heard the sound of a car outside. Undoubtedly only one person around here possessed such a high-powered car. It was Craig! As he came striding across the grass, he looked beautifully groomed in immaculate dark suit and snow-white shirt. Sandra wanted to hide or run away, do anything but have to face this well-dressed man looking as she did now, hot, sticky, and still dressed in her bikini and beach wrap.

Fortunately Vi saw him and went out to greet him.

'Craig, how nice to see you. What are you doing here?'

'I've come to fetch Sandra. I had hoped she would dine with me.'

'You must be joking,' said Sandra, emerging from the kitchen, wiping her sticky hands on her beach wrap and brushing back her streaked honey-gold hair. 'If I remember right, I said I wouldn't be able to come.'

'And I said I never take no for an answer if I've really set my heart on something.'

'You should have told me you were going out,' said Vi. 'We've had a bit of a domestic upset, Craig. These things happen in the best regulated households at times.'

'But . . . but I can't possibly go with you now.'

'Of course you can,' Vi asserted. 'Run along and change, Sandra. Craig can put up with my company for a wee while.'

'Yes,' Craig assented. 'Aunt Vi can give me some of that wonderful lemonade.'

Sandra was overruled by the two of them and went to have a quick shower. Anyhow, she reflected ruefully, she could hardly hesitate over which dress she should wear. A simple white dress was the only one she had that was suitable for dining out, but with its gold belt and the gold sandals she had bought at a shop sale some time ago, it would have to do. Julie had handed over some gilt ear-rings that she herself had tired of, and Sandra hesitated a little before putting them on. They swung from delicate chains and looked like small lanterns, giving her a more sophisticated appearance than usual. Brushing her damp gold hair and catching it up at the back with a filigree hair clasp, she glanced anxiously at herself in the mirror and was pleasantly surprised by her own reflection.

It was not often she had the chance to dress up. What a pity she had had to do it in such a hurry! She did not herself realize that the total effect was charming. The white dress set off the deep honey gold of her arms and legs and the low cut of the neckline showed the youthful tender curves of her slight figure. When she returned to the two who were drinking lemonade, there was a whistle of admiration from Craig, and Vi smiled approvingly.

She felt curiously shy to meet Craig's eyes, those eyes that could look so stormy, but, as she glanced timidly at him, were now full of sparkling laughter.

'You look rather lovely, my dear, doesn't she, Aunt Vi?'

Was he saying this to please her aunt, she wondered, or was he trying to make up for his previous ill humour? Now that the die was cast and she was going with him she felt a curious mixture of emotions. She could not help feeling thrilled at the idea of having an evening out with a man who could be charming however difficult she found him at times. And the idea of having a dinner that she had not supervised was also rather delightful. But in addition to these ordinary considerations there was something else, something that she did not quite understand, a tremulous feeling, half joy, half fear.

She had brought with her a rose-pink fluffy woollen wrap, but the weather was so mild for the time of the year that she hardly needed it, for it was almost like a summer's evening. They drove along the wide modern highway that had been built to link the small resorts along the coast. On each side were rolling fields of sugar cane, their silvery green leaves shimmering into gold in the light of the setting sun, and every now and again the road ran beside the sea where waves crashed on to lonely beaches or it skirted a group of small cottages beside a sedge-bordered lagoon.

'Do you remember what this was like before the road was built?' asked Craig. 'Though I suppose you're too young to recall it.'

'No, it's only been during the last few years that the place has developed to this extent. I suppose the new road was both the cause and effect in a way. I hardly think you yourself would have been interested in developing Fair Waves if your visitors had had to negotiate the road as it used to be. It was full of potholes, practically impassable in rainy weather. We were always breaking springs on the old Ford we had.'

'That's interesting ... and in spite of these conditions people came to spend holidays here in your aunt's hotel?'

'Yes, but. . . .'

Sandra hesitated. She could hardly be rude to Craig when she was his guest, but she must give an answer to his question.

'The people who used to come to our hotel were a different type of person from the ones who come to yours. They still are, in fact, though we're losing our old customers all the time, because they prefer to go to the Wild Coast now which is still, as they say, comparatively unspoiled.'

'I don't see why the building of a large beautiful hotel and good-looking chalets should be considered to spoil a coastline when the erection of any number of ramshackle cottages has been hitherto considered legitimate. But I'm sorry if the fact that I've developed the place has led to Aunt Vi losing her customers.'

It was not worth arguing, Sandra felt. She did not want to spoil the pleasure of the evening by going over all the troubles that had beset them since Craig's hotel was built. After all, it was not his fault that they lacked capital and that their hotel was sadly out of step with modern trends. He had only hastened a state of affairs which would have probably caught up with them sooner or later.

'This road takes the same course as the old elephant road,' she said, trying to change the subject. 'Did you know? It's the trail that the elephants used long ago when they used to trek in search of food and water. A hundred years ago you could see them in the forest on the high ridge above the bay where now there's a city.'

Craig smiled at this and Sandra wondered whether she had sounded too pedantic. Certainly Julie would never start giving a man she was determined to charm a lecture about the early history of the country or about wild life.

No, Julie would be teasing him with that enchanting smile, engaging him in light chatter. But Sandra felt she was not the type to be successful at this kind of thing, especially not with Craig. He was watching the road, his large brown hands lightly touching the wheel, but now he glanced at her, meeting her look with a mischievous grin.

'So do you wish that the elephants were still upon the ridge and down below where there's the city there were still dark green mangrove trees and swampy ground? If there had been no development by your forefathers, it would have still been wild sub-tropical bush for most of the way along the coast.'

'Of course I do realize there must be some development, Craig. I'm not as conservative as to wish everything to remain a wilderness, but sometimes I wish it hadn't happened to our village. I suppose I'm being terribly selfish.'

'I suppose you'll be very disapproving if I tell you that soon I intend to take a ride up the coast with Manoel to investigate the possibility of opening up another resort. Of course it very much depends upon our success here whether we do this, but there would be no harm in getting an option on the land.'

Sandra did not tell him that she already knew about this plan from Julie and that he intended to take Julie and her mother with him. She fully realized that his invitation for this evening arose from a desire to make up for his harshness concerning the swimming lesson and also to show his gratitude for her help when Kim was swept out to sea. The fact that he had asked Julie to join them in the trip up the coast showed clearly where his interests lay.

'I don't suppose it makes much difference whether I approve or not, Craig.'

Craig smiled a little wryly.

'Frankly, Sandra, it doesn't. My business commitments are too complicated at the moment to leave room for sentiment. But don't let's be like this with each other. Let's enjoy this evening.'

He took his hand from the wheel and stroked her arm, then took her hand in his very gently. When he smiled like that and his grey eyes softened as they looked into hers she could forgive him for all her ruffled emotions. But wasn't it less dangerous if she kept up her feelings of animosity towards him?

Along the coast but a little way inland there was a small hamlet that owed its beauty to the fact that long ago the owners of a sugar estate had designed their employees' cottages to look like old Cape Dutch houses. The public buildings were beautiful, white, gabled and set amongst green sweeping lawns with sparkling fountains. Everywhere one looked there were different colours of bougainvillea in full flower, pink, magenta, bronze, scarlet.

They drove through the little town and came to a gabled house on a high rise overlooking the distant sea. This restaurant had been a private house and it still had the intimate atmosphere of an old distinguished home. The circular tables set in secluded nooks of the dining room were of early Victorian design with pedestal legs and tops of inlaid rosewood, and the bustle-back dining room chairs were covered in ruby velvet. The panelled walls were made brighter by hunting prints and the china rail held gleaming copper jugs and blue and white Delft plates. The lighting was subdued and soft music came from some hidden source. Since it was mid-week, the place was not crowded. To Sandra it seemed beautifully quiet and peaceful after the hustle of serving meals at Wave Crest.

They sat in a small alcove furnished with small antique settees surrounding low tables. The small sofas enforced a close intimacy because they were only meant for two people.

'Aren't these known as "love seats"?' asked Craig, putting his arm along the back of the settee in order to get room to sit. 'Now I understand why.'

'No, love seats are the ones that face opposite directions.'

Craig laughed. 'That would be more appropriate for us, wouldn't it, Sandra?'

He ordered Martinis. 'Good girl,' he commented

when Sandra expressed a preference for a dry one. 'I see we share the same tastes.'

While they were drinking the cocktails, they contemplated the large menu.

'How about oysters?' asked Craig.

Sandra shuddered.

'No, I'm afraid our tastes don't coincide as much as that, but please eat them yourself. I'll try not to look.'

Craig had a dozen oysters with brown bread and butter cut delicately thin, while Sandra had a seafood cocktail, and this course was followed by a delicious filet en croute, tender meat with a mushroom sauce, cooked in a little castle of crisp pastry. With this they drank an excellent claret, then finally came an orange soufflé, light as sea foam. It was so good to eat food one had not supervised oneself, thought Sandra, and she said as much to Craig.

'I like a girl to have a healthy-appetite,' he commented, but Sandra thought this could apply even more so to Julie, who could usually eat more heartily than herself.

Between courses they danced in the small space left in the middle of the room and Sandra found that her steps fitted naturally with Craig's slightly old-fashioned style of dancing. She could not imagine him doing the hectic type of dancing that they practised at the discothèque, and yet if this had been Julie with him she supposed he would have followed her tastes. This thought made Sandra feel slightly depressed, but she tried to think that she must enjoy this evening without thought of the future.

It was very easy to talk to Craig, but then doubtless he was very experienced in being sociable with all kinds of girls.

93

'It's lovely here,' she smiled up at him as they sat down again. 'I'm enjoying the evening so much. It isn't often one goes to a quiet place these days.'

Craig smiled.

'A quiet place isn't necessarily profitable, Sandra, enjoyable as you may find it. These days people demand something more lively. They like to eat to the accompaniment of a band or at least to loud music. You don't often find people who prefer a quiet place. Your generation has been brought up to be accustomed to a background of pop music.'

'Is that why your hotel seems popular, because you have lots of gay music?'

'We hope to cater for public demand. I have to think of my profits.'

Oh dear, thought Sandra, however much she tried to introduce other subjects they always seemed to come back to that of profit and loss.

'Do you never think of anything else but making money?' she asked, and then wished the words unsaid, for she had been determined to be agreeable to Craig for this one evening.

Craig frowned. 'I have to, strange as it may seem to you. I realize that my hotel and the other enterprises look as if they're doing enormously well, but it's early days yet and everything depends on the success of this season. I've sunk all my capital into this one venture. If the hotel doesn't succeed . . . and you must realize what an enormous expenditure it takes to keep it going . . . I'll go under.'

Sandra was amazed. She had thought of Craig as a very wealthy man and she still supposed that he was, but apparently everything did not come as easily as that.

'Life in the hotel world is always a bit of a gamble, as you know, Sandra. And the more you put into it, the more you stand to lose. However, don't let's be gloomy. There's no need, I assure you. The hotel is thriving at the moment.'

'Which is more than can be said for ours,' said Sandra.

'That's another thing that concerns me. I'd like to help Aunt Vi by putting some capital into her place or even offering to take over, but at the moment my hands are tied. Every bit of capital I own is sunk into this one venture. Of course the house took too much as well. Perhaps next year if you can hold out as long I might be able to do something.'

A few days ago Sandra would have been indignant at the idea of Craig's patronage, but now her feelings had undergone a change. She felt more in sympathy with him because he had explained his difficulties, and a Craig to whom everything did not come so easily was a more attractive man than the arrogant, apparently wealthy person she had first met.

As they drove home, a full moon was painting a path of silver across the dark azure sea and the little sandy beaches glittered whitely. There were very few cars on the road and the small hamlets they passed through were unilluminated. The quietness of the sleeping countryside emphasized the intimate atmosphere in the small space of the car with the light of the dashboard showing Craig's dark profile.

It seemed to Sandra that she was travelling on a road to nowhere with a mysterious stranger. How much did she know about this man, actually? He had come into her life totally unexpectedly and had aroused feelings of dislike at first, but now, unwilling as she was to admit it, he seemed to be taking over too large a part of her innermost thoughts. She told herself she must fight against the tender emotions that rose unbidden when he looked at her with that melting smile.

'Light a cigarette for me, will you?' he asked, and her hands trembled as she cupped them around the flame. But his request had served to distract her thoughts.

'It's refreshing to find a girl who doesn't chatter the whole time,' he commented.

Sandra wondered whether this was a veiled criticism. Her company could not be as welcome as Julie's with her animated vivacity. She was alarmed to find herself wishing that this drive could last longer. Soon they would be home and she did not expect this experience would ever be repeated, for she felt she had been dull company and had argued about contentious issues when she would have been well advised to remain silent and had not talked when it would have been better to try to be entertaining.

Only one or two outside lights were burning when they arrived back at Wave Crest. There were sleepy cluckings from the direction of the bird cages and the mahem cranes were giving their characteristic sound, a deep booming note, 'Mahem, mahem'. Craig got out of the car and opened the door for Sandra. She held out her hand.

'Thank you for a lovely evening.'

Craig laughed. In the moonlight, his face was dark and a little sinister, something like the pirate Julie had described.

'You're like a little girl saying thank you for her first party. But you're not a little girl. You're a very attractive woman. Don't you realize that?'

She was in his arms and his kiss was long and demanding, but, even as she felt her senses responding to this dark frightening stranger, a small voice of common sense said, he does this with every woman he takes out to dinner because he things it's expected of a man with his reputation. It's Julie who interests him really.

She broke away and tried to speak coolly.

'From the first day we met, Craig, you've shown that you like to make love to any girl you happen to be alone with. I must be very attracted to a man before I let him kiss me.'

'And you're not attracted to me?'

'Not in that way.'

He gave a short laugh.

'A pity, that. It couldn't happen that you're lying, Sandra, could it? But no, that so cool expression leads me to think the girl is telling the truth.'

He looked into her eyes and she found she could not speak, but shook her head as if to deny the emotion she was afraid must be all too evident to his keen gaze even by moonlight. But in a moment he had turned his back upon her. She watched him stride swiftly back to the car and was still standing motionless as a statue in her white dress when the purr of the engine died away on the woodland road.

CHAPTER SEVEN

A week had passed since Sandra had had dinner with Craig and although she continued to give lessons to Kim at the house she had not once seen him. She could not think that her repudiation of his embrace had seriously worried him and she did not think it was important enough to him to make her avoid her. Kim had told her that he was tremendously busy and she had grumbled that he seldom had dinner at home now, but Sandra could not help wondering whether this was because he was seeking Julie's company. Certainly she herself saw very little of her friend these days.

She felt sad that the pleasant dinner had had such a difficult ending, but she had not realized that her depression had shown so clearly as she went about the usual tasks of housekeeping for the hotel until one morning when Vi said, 'Why don't you give yourself a treat this morning? Go and buy a new dress with some of the money you're earning. I refuse to take all of it to go towards our expenses. It's like trying to stop a leak in the dyke with one's thumb. Have a bit of pleasure for once. You work too hard and you're looking quite peaky.'

Sandra protested that she was quite all right, but Vi when she had made up her mind about something was not to be gainsaid. So Sandra found herself driving the old Ford into the village and parking it near Julie's mother's boutique.

Buying a dress was quite a problem since it must be useful for any occasion practically. It was quite difficult to find this kind of dress at the boutique as Mrs. Burnett stocked the exotic kind of gown that might be presumed to appeal to wealthy holidaymakers, such as dresses with bright stripes, glamorous culotte suits, beaded evening dresses. But since Sandra was Julie's friend, Mrs. Burnett was kind and did not attempt to press upon her any of the more expensive kind of clothes that she imported from Europe.

'I know exactly what you need,' she told Sandra. 'Now let's see.' She ran her hands along the racks. 'I think I have just the very thing. It only came in yesterday.'

It was a cream dress in a dull silky material like shantung, but it was made of one of the polyester fibres and was therefore crease-resisting. Very simple yet beautifully cut, it had a detachable scarf of green, gold and light brown. It was the kind of dress that would look good with costume jewellery for the evening, but with a scarf it would do very well for a day in town. And it fitted Sandra as if it had been specially made for her.

She could not help thinking, if only I had had this for my dinner date with Craig, for it showed up the gold-streaked warm brown hair and the honey-gold of her arms and legs. The brown in the scarf seemed to emphasize the colour of her eyes.

'Oh, Sandra, you look gorgeous!' exclaimed Julie as she bounced into the shop with Manoel in tow. 'Why didn't you show it to me first, Mum?'

Mrs. Burnett smiled fondly.

'You aren't the tailored type, love. You need something a bit more glam. Besides, this is an all-purpose dress and there's no need for you to think about economizing. Specially not now.'

What did she mean by that? Sandra wondered. And yet it was obvious she was thinking of Craig's interest in her daughter. Yet Julie still seemed to keep Manoel's interest. But then she always did have a lot of admirers.

'Do you know what Manoel heard on the beach, Mum? Can I tell her?'

'I suppose so,' Manoel replied a trifle grudgingly. 'But it's not a story I want to get about. I told those two surfies to keep quiet about it. However, I suppose your mother is safe and Sandra would certainly not want to spread it around for her own sake.'

'These two said that sharks have been sighted every day for the past week just off shore. And they say they're the Zambesi type, the kind responsible for those shark attacks some years ago.'

'I haven't heard anything about this before,' said Sandra. 'Are you sure it's true? Did they actually see them, or was it someone else?'

'I'm sure it's just a rumour,' said Manoel hastily. 'And it's an ugly rumour. We can't afford that it should get around, and neither can you, Miss Hamilton. Once that kind of thing gets into the national newspapers it's tickets for the hotel trade this season.'

'But how can you stop it? And what if it's true?'

'I'm sure it's not true. Even if it is the sharks aren't likely to come close inshore. You can only stifle this kind of tale by not letting the local newspapermen get hold of it.'

'That means Gary,' said Sandra. 'You'd better not tell him, Julie.'

Julie shrugged indifferently.

'I never see him these days. He's all yours, Sandra.'

Sandra had been away from the beach for some time while she had been giving swimming lessons to Kim, so she could not judge what truth there was in these stories. She was sure an alarm would be raised soon enough if sharks were sighted. Some years ago there had been a series of shark attacks upon bathers all along the coast and since then the larger resorts had had shark nets lowered into the water, but for a small place the cost of installing and maintaining them was exorbitant. On the other hand, even the rumour of sharks in the vicinity could ruin the whole season. In fact during the previous scare many small hotels had not been able to weather the cancellation of bookings and the fall in income.

This was one of the reasons that Craig had installed his hotel's luxurious Olympic-sized swimming pool, but even so the interest in surfing and skin-diving had grown so much that people wanted to be able to swim in the sea without fear of attack. It was useless for experts to point out the fact that there were hundreds of deaths on the road every year and the incidence of death by shark attack was minimal compared with this. The horror of such a happening and the sensationalism with which the newspapers treated it was enough to scare away potential holidaymakers from the place where it had occurred.

Sandra hoped these rumours could be scotched before they grew to alarming proportions. There were always sharks around, but well out to sea. It was unlikely that they would come into the breakers amongst the bathers. At all costs Gary must not print anything about it. It was difficult to know what to do about this. He might not have heard anything and it would be foolish to draw his attention to it by asking him not to write about it.

Thinking these thoughts, she was not over-pleased when Gary came to her after lunch.

'Hi, Sandra. How about coming up the river with me this afternoon? Someone has lent me a canoe and I plan on taking some photographs in the late afternoon light. It's all good publicity for the place, you know, if I can get them printed, and it's a bit of a boost for me.'

'I'm sorry, Gary, I'll be giving Kim a swimming lesson.'

'Not for the whole afternoon, surely. I don't mind taking the kid too. She would enjoy it, wouldn't she?'

'Yes,' Sandra agreed a little doubtfully. Would Craig like her to take his precious daughter on such an expedition? But there would be no harm in it. And Kim was indeed a poor little rich girl. She did not get many treats like this.

'We can see if she would like to,' Sandra compromised.

'Good. Then I'll call for you at the house, right?'

'No, don't do that. We'll meet you at the landing stage.'

Gary grinned a little wryly, 'What gives? Are you trying to keep me away from his lordship's palace? He's mighty cagy about letting anyone see it, isn't he? Does he keep a harem there or something?'

Kim, of course, was delighted with the idea and after the swimming lesson they left a message with the servants in case Craig arrived to visit her and met Gary at the landing stage as arranged.

'Hi, Kim, what a glamorous costume! Aren't I the lucky chap to be able to take two lovely girls with me?' said Gary.

He seemed to set himself out to be charming to the young girl, chatting away to her as if he had known her all his life.

'Craig always says I mustn't talk to newspapermen, but this is different, isn't it, Sandra?'

Sandra felt a small qualm of doubt. She had for the moment forgotten about Craig's strict rules about possible publicity concerning his home life. But this was just a harmless afternoon's excursion. Gary could hardly make anything of this. Nevertheless she must have a word with him about it later.

It was delightful skimming up river in the little craft. Reeds bordered the sides and sometimes there hung upon them groups of round nests made by the yellow and green weaver birds. Pied black and white kingfishers quartered the water, diving every now and again for their prey, and water turtles sat on the banks in the golden light of the late afternoon sun with legs splayed and heads raised to catch its gentle warmth.

Gary had brought light fishing rods and they fished with not very much success, although in the still waters they could see fish jumping out after midges, then falling back with a resounding splash. It was probably Kim's chatter that put them off, for Sandra had seldom seen the little girl so animated. She seemed to have taken a fancy to Gary and he was sweet with her, laughing, joking, sometimes teasing her.

This is what she needs, she thought. She doesn't get enough of Craig's company. But then it's very difficult for him. If he marries Julie what will happen to Kim? Sandra could not imagine that Julie would want a ready-made daughter.

'Oh, look, there's Craig!' exclaimed Kim when they were some way from the landing stage on their way back. Sandra was annoyed to feel her heart beating a little faster at the sight of that tall figure silhouetted blackly against the light of the setting sun. She hoped that he did not disapprove of Kim's little jaunt and had come to tell her so. But when they drew up beside the jetty he responded with a smiling face to Kim's excited chatter.

'Don't you wish you could have come, Craig? We had such a super time. We fished, but we didn't catch anything, and we saw turtles and Gary took photographs. Don't you think Gary's a super boy-friend for Sandra? I'm so glad she has such a nice one, aren't you? You do go steady with him, don't you, Sandra?'

It was just as well Gary was still busy with the business of beaching the canoe, otherwise Sandra could imagine his hoots of mirth.

'You've made Sandra blush now, Kim,' said Craig.

It was not Kim's statement but Craig's speculative glance that had confused Sandra, but she could hardly say so.

'Thank you for letting Kim join in your expedition, Sandra,' said Craig. 'And please thank your young man too. We must be going now, Kim.'

Kim had to skip to match Craig's swift stride. Sandra rejoined Gary, who was still wiping the sand from the boat's fittings.

'Quite a nice kid,' he commented. 'An improvement on the father, I must say.'

Sandra was so confused by her encounter with Craig that she forgot about her intention to warn Gary off publicity where Kim was concerned. How was it that Craig's dark brooding glance could raise a storm of emotion in her heart that she neither wanted nor sought? And why did she feel hurt at his calm assumption that Gary was her boy-friend?

It was some days later that Julie phoned, sounding rather perturbed. 'Sandra darling, something dreadful has happened. We're supposed to be going up the coast with Craig tomorrow and now Mum has a heavy cold and says she can't come. She won't hear of my going alone with Craig and Manoel. She has such old-fashioned ideas sometimes.'

'What a pity, Julie. I know you were looking forward to it. What will you do?'

'Mum suggested that you and Aunt Vi might like to go in her place.'

Sandra was astounded.

'I don't think Craig would like that arrangement at all.'

'Why not? He likes Aunt Vi. I've heard him say so. And he must be well disposed to you if he allows you to give swimming lessons to his brat.'

'Yes, but this is different. Besides, I don't think we could both be away from the hotel at the same time, even though we aren't very busy at the moment.'

'Yes, I said as much to Mum. I thought you would say that. But, Sandra, I persuaded Mum that if Aunt Vi can't come we should go on our own. There's safety in numbers, and in any case Mum said she would trust you to keep me in order. She has a nerve, I must say. Do you fancy yourself in the role of chaperon, Sandra?'

No, thought Sandra, I can't say I do, especially the idea of being chaperon to Craig and Julie. On the other hand, it would be very exciting to go for the trip up the coast, a lovely change from the hotel chores.

And she would be able to look after Kim and see that she did not feel too neglected while Craig paid attention to Julie. She did not care for Manoel very much. But still she might be able to avoid his company. In any case he would be talking business with Craig most of the time, she hoped.

'How long are you going to be away?' she asked.

'Only one night. Do come, Sandra, there's a dear.'

'I'll have to talk it over with Vi,' Sandra told her.

But Vi was very agreeable to the plan and Julie arranged it with Craig. Sandra wondered what his reaction had been, but evidently it had been favourable, although he did not phone to confirm this.

The next day when they set out, Sandra was not surprised when Julie took her place in the comfortable front passenger seat as if by right, though she noticed Kim gave her a scowling glance. The child said nothing, however, and took her place between Manoel and Sandra in the large back seat of the powerful car.

The road wound along the coast for some way and then plunged inland amongst sweeping fields of sugar cane. The land was hilly and as far as the eye could see there was the pale green cane with its reedy fronds trembling in the soft breeze like waves of the sea. There were spacious white homesteads built upon the higher slopes where they could catch any cool breezes in the long hot days of the humid summer. Bougainvilleas rioted in the hedges along the roadside, magenta and scarlet, and the bright orange golden shower lived up to its name, hanging like a gilded waterfall from the tall trees.

They halted for breakfast at a wayside inn that was a

motel and café in one, and found that it was warm enough already to sit out at the table in the paved court-yard in the bright winter sunlight.

'The announcer said on the radio that there's snow in the mountains, but you would never think so here,' said Craig, shedding his lovat tweed jacket and revealing a dark green polo-necked shirt.

Manoel kept on his corduroy turquoise jacket, declaring that he did not think it was so warm. His glamorous appearance, the silky well-groomed hair and the rather pale skin with his ultra-fashionable clothes were a strange contrast to Craig's cleancut looks, Sandra thought. It was queer that two such different men should be able to run a hotel, working in harmony together. Manoel did not seem so difficult to get on with after all. She was in a different position now with him than when she had been trying to get a job at the hotel. Since she was Craig's guest the manager was going out of his way to be exceptionally charming, and Sandra was grateful for this even if as she surmised it meant very little and was mostly for Julie's benefit anyway.

They were very ready for the sizzling lamb chops that were brought to them on a platter together with crisp golden fried eggs and grilled tomatoes. Kim was the only one reluctant to eat.

Julie yawned.

'I still haven't got over the shock to my system of getting up so early,' she moaned.

Nevertheless she ate a hearty breakfast. She had always had a slight tendency to put on weight and now, with the constant rich food that she ate at the hotel in the evenings in the course of her work, her curves were a little too pronounced. But otherwise she looked lovely. She was wearing a chalk-white slacks suit, a little on the tight side, but it was a good foil for her glowing radiant brown skin and black shining hair. The extra weight suited her in a way in that it gave her an air of sleekness and wellbeing.

Sandra in her navy slacks and ribbed white sweater looked a little too slender on the other hand. She had been used to playing second fiddle to Julie's beauty for a long time and had never felt jealous of the other girl's more spectacular looks, but this morning, with Craig responding teasingly to Julie's vivacity, she envied the ease that beauty of Julie's kind brought with it.

Kim regarded Julie's lovely laughing face with some disfavour.

'Aren't you afraid all those pieces of toast will make you get fatter?' she said. 'That slacks suit is a bit tight already.'

Julie frowned and then quickly recovered her self-possession. Sandra felt she would have shown her annoyance more if she had not wanted to impress Craig. She could not help admiring her self-control.

'If it does get too tight, I can buy another one. Plenty more where this came from.'

'It's very rude to make personal remarks. You're a little old for that, Kim,' Craig reproved. 'Julie looks perfectly delightful as always.'

Julie turned to Craig with her enchanting smile.

'Just for that, Craig darling, I'll give you a kiss, even at this time in the morning.'

She put her arms around his neck and kissed him lingeringly. Kim could scarcely restrain her disgust, and Sandra, thinking it was time to intervene, tactfully suggested that she and Kim should go to the rest room before resuming the journey.

'She's so stupid,' Kim protested as she splashed water around the place in her desire to give vent to her feelings. 'I don't know how she can be your friend, Sandra.'

'She isn't stupid, Kim. You're just being a little silly because Craig is being friendly towards her. She's a very charming person really. You must try to like her, since Craig does. And you must admit she's very beautiful.'

'Goodness, do you think so?' asked Kim. 'I don't think she's half as beautiful as you, Sandra.'

What odd standards children have, thought Sandra. If they like a person then that person appears beautiful to them, however they really look.

'You're being rather flattering, Kim, and I appreciate it, but it isn't exactly true, I'm afraid.'

'It is true, and anyhow you have a much better figure than her. She's much too fat.'

'But it's very becoming.'

But Kim was adamant.

'She's artificial, with her false eyelashes and all that eye make-up. If you did yourself up like that you'd look twice as beautiful as her.'

There was no arguing with Kim when she had made up her obstinate little mind and Sandra was forced to give up, but she thought it did not augur well for the future. She would have to see what she could do to persuade Kim to change her opinion of Julie as it seemed Craig was really interested in her.

Craig had arranged that they should stay the night at a place run by the Parks Board beside a lake that was near the sea, although the lake itself was of fresh water. When they arrived in midmorning there was still a translucent look about the scene. The vast lake was still and calm, its opalescent waters stretching as far as the eye could see with no glimpse of the further shore, for it was still hidden by the heavy morning mist. There was a sense of brooding tranquillity that seemed not quite of this world.

They were to sleep in neat white huts furnished simply but adequately with beds, built-in cupboards and small refrigerators. They had brought their own supply of food, but an African employed by the camp would cook it in a central kitchen. Craig and Manoel set off almost immediately to go to see the land that was offered for sale in this vicinity, leaving Sandra and Julie to settle down but taking Kim with them. Sandra suspected that Craig wanted to make up to the little girl for his neglect of her during the last weeks. All her ill temper seemed to be forgotten as she went off in the car, beaming with joy as she commandeered the front seat.

Sandra busied herself sorting out the supplies for the meals. Julie watched her for a few minutes without offering to help, then started to change into her white bikini.

'I think I'll catch a bit of sun while it's still hot,' she said. 'Come soon, Sandra. I hate being alone. I don't know why Craig had to go off on this silly business jag straight away.'

'Well, since that's the cause of the trip, it seems quite reasonable.'

Julie looked with disfavour at the tins and supplies that Sandra was sorting.

'Surely they don't expect us to eat here! I'd expected we would dine at the hotel. In fact I didn't know why Craig chose to stay in this place at all. Why couldn't we have stayed at the hotel in the first place?'

There was a small hotel in the village nearby, but it was in the small dusty main street.

'I think Craig probably thought this kind of place would be a pleasant change. He must get pretty sick of hotels.'

'Change or not,' grumbled Julie, 'when he comes back I'm going to ask him to take me to the hotel this evening. Even in a one-horse place like this there's probably something happening on a Saturday night.'

But it seemed her bad mood was over when they were all sitting in front of the huts in the warm winter sunlight enjoying drinks before lunch. The lake was directly in front of them and pelicans were landing with accurate precision like flying boats sliding to a halt on the still waters. On a sandbank, hippos basked, their pinkish stomachs exposed to the mild rays of the sun, and flamingoes dug in the shallows with their curiously hooked beaks or rose suddenly like a cloud of bright pink blossom as they showed the undersides of their wings.

This all gave promise of fascinating glimpses of wild life and Sandra had a great longing to go out upon the lake to see more, so she was pleased when Craig said, 'I've arranged to hire a boat to use later this afternoon. How will you like that, Kim?'

'Super,' said Kim, who seemed tireless as far as expeditions with Craig were concerned.

At the same time, Julie, who had been talking to Manoel, turned to the others, saying, 'Manoel has just been telling me there's quite a decent little swimming bath at the hotel and there should be an amusing crowd of visitors. How about going over this afternoon, Craig? I've had about enough of this nature in the raw, haven't you?'

'I'm afraid not, Julie. I was just telling Kim and Sandra that I've hired a launch for the afternoon.'

Julie smiled persuasively.

'But you can cancel it, I guess. It will be much more fun at the hotel. What's the point of riding around the lake anyway?'

'I had hoped to take a ciné of wild life, or at least see if there is any. I must know what to promise visitors if I do build a hotel in the neighbourhood.'

Julie pouted prettily.

'Can't you leave Sandra and Kim to take your movies for you? I'm sure Sandra would be delighted, and a game guard can drive the launch.'

Craig frowned.

'I'm afraid not, Julie. I promised Kim I would take her.'

Kim, who had been listening to this conversation rather apprehensively, smiled in a relieved way and it was Julie's turn to frown.

'Well,' she said petulantly, 'we don't all have to be bored, do we? Manoel will take me to the hotel, won't you, darling?'

'Certainly,' Manoel assented eagerly. 'That is, if you don't need me, Craig. I must confess I'm not a great one for the wild life myself either.'

'Then that's settled,' said Craig equably.

Sandra was surprised that he took Julie's ill temper so calmly. It seemed that even if he was in love with her, he did not intend that she should have all her own way.

'Kim and Sandra, you can have a rest after lunch, but don't make it too long. We must be on the water to see the birds come in near sunset.'

Craig took the wheel himself, when they were ready, and the sun-bronzed man who handled the launch so skilfully across the still waters of the lake seemed to Sandra an entirely different person from the sophisticated owner of the hotel, the stranger to whom at first she had felt so much animosity.

The boat did not move very fast, for Craig did not want to disturb the birds, and Sandra, sitting beside him, could observe his hands guiding the wheel with such ease and the clearcut profile with that lock of dark hair, and the mouth that had seemed so hard, smiling and gentle now as he listened to some remark of Kim's.

She was glad he had handed her the fieldglasses, for she could use them to disguise her own expression. She was afraid she would show her pleasure too much, the feeling of joy that welled up in her heart when she was in his company. For hard as she fought against this emotion it was there waiting to overwhelm her if she thought about it too deeply.

She realized with a bitter pang that he did not even particularly like her. Everything that he had done, any friendliness he had shown towards her, was not for her own sake, but because she had done some good to his daughter or because he had taken a liking to Vi and wanted to help her. He had tried to make love to her, yes, but this was only because the girls by whom he was normally surrounded in his hotel trade appeared to expect this kind of thing from a personable man. It had nothing to do with any feeling he might have for herself. Indeed, she did not think he had any such emotion except one of mild curiosity that a girl could express such odd opinions as she did.

Their lives, their very way of thinking, were miles

apart. An impenetrable gap separated the kind of life she liked to lead and the way that he had chosen. He seemed to adore wealth and power, and she liked the simple life she had led so far with Vi in the little unpretentious hotel beside the sea.

But now for one afternoon he seemed to be a different person as they glided over the lake in the late afternoon, the lake that was shimmering now with the colours of shot silk as flocks of white egrets winged their way home to perch like white pear blossom on the leafless trees. Cormorants with snakelike necks took up their places upon the posts beside the landing stages, forsaking the fishing they had practised all day to assuage their own never-ending appetite. In the rosy light they looked like birds in a Japanese painting.

On the further shore they could see hippos disporting themselves in the shallow water. They had been sleeping on the wet sand in the heat of the afternoon and now they were lively and playful with each other before they came up on to the banks to graze for their evening meal.

Craig hardly spoke except to answer some question put by Kim. The whir of the ciné camera seemed loud in the still air, and sounds like the splash of water upon the bow and the call of a bird or a hippo's grunt sounded very clearly.

'Will you bring people to the lake if you build a hotel here?' asked Kim.

'Yes, that's the idea,' said Craig. 'But we would need larger launches to accommodate more people at once.'

'But aren't you afraid,' asked Sandra, 'that if you brought more people here, the birds and animals would become more shy and go further away or desert this place?'

'No, I'm hoping they would get used to people, just as the animals have in the Kruger National Park.'

'I would hate to see this lovely place over-commercialized. It would be ghastly to have curio shops and restaurants.'

'We could reserve that kind of thing for the hotel itself.'

'A monopoly, in fact,' Sandra commented.

'Yes, why not? We need all the money we can get to help pay expenses.'

Sandra was just contemplating some biting retort when the launch's engine made a rumbling noise, gave a prolonged cough and then was silent.

'What the devil . . .?' said Craig, frowning.

He made several attempts to start the engine, but it remained obstinately silent, or else gave a few hiccups that died out in seconds. The lake was calm, but the drift of the water and wind seemed to direct them slowly and inexorably towards a sandbank where several large crocodiles were basking, in the last rays of sunlight.

'We can't go in there, Craig!' shouted Kim in alarm. 'Look at those crocs!'

'There are a couple of oars there,' said Craig. 'Sandra, can you try to row while I have another go at the engine?'

Sandra took the oars. There was a strong current here and she had to row against it, but the sight of the crocodiles with their evil grins plainly visible was enough incentive to use every bit of strength she had. She seemed to make no progress, however, and realized that they were getting nearer to the bank, although the pace of their approach had slackened a little.

Craig looked up from his struggle with the engine.

'For God's sake, Sandra, can't you row any better than that!'

The feeling of happiness she had experienced with Craig during the last tranquil hour vanished and she felt again the burning resentment she was so accustomed to have in her dealings with this exasperating man.

'It's impossible,' she gasped. 'And you are too!'

'Give me the oars,' he said, taking no notice of her resentment so loudly expressed, and he poled them away from the dangerous spot in such an easy fashion that Sandra wondered why he had not done it in the first place. She reflected ruefully that he would never have expected such a feat of strength from Julie.

Just then the sound of a hail came over the water, and there was a large Parks Board launch speeding towards them.

'Hi there, do you need a tow?' the ranger asked, and in no time at all they were on their way back to the safer area of the camp.

'It wouldn't be funny to get left on one of those islets after sunset, or anywhere where there are crocs and hippos, for that matter,' said the ranger. 'It's a good thing we saw you.'

'Where on earth have you been?' asked Julie. 'What kept you?'

But she barely listened to their explanations, for she was brimming over with enthusiasm about the gay crowd they had met at the hotel.

'We said we'd go back to the dance this evening,' she informed Craig. 'Of course you'll come, Craig darling. Sandra won't mind looking after Kim, will you?'

'Not at all,' said Sandra, forestalling any objection Kim might raise. After all, she had come as an extra person with the sole purpose of being useful, so she had better make the best of it, and after Craig's brusque behaviour in the last hour, she would be glad to have a rest from his company.

'Then that's that,' said Julie. 'Sandra isn't keen on dancing, anyhow, and Craig will probably meet local inhabitants who could be useful to him in his plans.'

So after supper Julie went off with the two men. She was looking lovely as usual in a bright red and white dress, short and swirling, and bright red sandals. At the last minute she picked a hibiscus and put it in her hair that she had twisted into a curly knot above her brow.

Sandra spent the evening playing double patience with Kim until the child started to yawn and could keep awake no longer. Sandra was sharing the room with her and Julie and she could not keep the light on to read while Kim was going to sleep, so she turned it off and went to sit outside upon a bench on the bank above the lake.

Below she could hear the sounds of a hippo munching at the weedy growth by the water's edge and there were sleepy cluckings from the reeds. The moon had risen and was tracing a path of silver over the calm waters. She sat there trying not to think of Craig dancing with Julie, who would be looking enchanting and coquettish with the scarlet hibiscus in her silky dark hair.

She tried instead to think of practical things like how they were to manage for another season if they did not get more bookings and how she could economize further with regard to the menus while at the same time not appearing ungenerous. But all the time these thoughts would disappear and instead there would be the image of Craig's dark face, the lock of hair that made him look younger than his years, the charming wicked smile that she could not forget, in spite of her exasperation of the afternoon.

There was the soft swish of footsteps upon dew-wet grass and Craig stood in front of her. He was so much a part of her thoughts that she looked dreamily at him as if he did not really exist.

'Wake up, Sandra. What are you doing here? Aren't you cold, my dear?'

'No,' said Sandra. She was trembling, but it was not caused by the cold. 'Here, have my jacket. I seem to make a habit of giving it to you, don't I?'

Once more she was enclosed in the warm tweedy coat before she could even protest.

'Where are the others?' she asked, bewildered.

'Manoel and Julie? Oh, don't worry about them. They're quite happy at the dance. They won't miss me.'

Sandra was puzzled. Had Julie gone too far in arousing Craig's jealousy towards Manoel? And why had Craig returned? She supposed she would hear the story tomorrow.

Meanwhile Craig sat beside her on the bench.

'Is the moonlit lake so much more interesting than me, Sandra?' he asked.

She turned slowly to meet his gaze.

'That's better. You are a strange girl. You seem to actually prefer your own company most of the time, don't you?'

'I don't mind my own company, but it's not true to say I prefer it.'

Craig slid his hand along the back of the bench, and held her gently.

'That's a concession, anyway. Are you glad to see me, Sandra?'

How could she answer? She met his smiling gaze with difficulty. Then all at once she was in his arms and he was kissing her with a demanding passion to which she felt her every sense responding, but she forced herself to slip from his grasp and stood up, then walked a few paces away, turning her back to him and facing the pewtery sheen of the lake as she fought for composure.

His hands were on her shoulders, his face in her soft hair.

'What is it, Sandra? Why are you so cold? Am I trespassing somewhere where I shouldn't be? Are you thinking of the young man in whose company I've so often seen you?'

Swiftly through her mind came the thought that he was flirting with her again as he appeared to do with most girls. Julie must have annoyed him in some way at the dance and he had come back determined to break down the barriers that she, Sandra, had raised when he had tried to make love to her on those two previous occasions. It would be best to let him think she was attracted to Gary, rather than admit as she longed to do that all her thoughts were centred upon himself.

'You're not free, is that it?' asked Craig, facing her now, his hands on her shoulders.

'No, I'm not free. Not free at all, Craig.'

Craig's hands fell to his sides.

'You can be sure of one thing, then, Sandra. In future I won't trouble you any more. I give you my word.'

119

CHAPTER EIGHT

NEXT morning when they were preparing for the return journey, Julie had gone out to talk to Manoel and Craig in the sunlight while Sandra, with Kim helping, packed the remaining food. Julie was in a good mood today.

'We had a fabulous time,' she informed Sandra. 'The hotel is pretty crummy, of course, but what could one expect for such a small place? But there was a bright crowd at the dance – all the local sugar-farming crowd. I was a bit peeved with Craig because he vanished for a while. I think he must have been a spot jealous because some of the other men were making a fuss of me. However, after a while he came back and we danced together for the rest of the evening.'

Sandra thought it was just as she had surmised. Craig had come back to the camp in a fit of pique, but then when Sandra had refused his flirtatious advances he had returned to Julie.

'I'm beginning to think you're right about Craig, Sandra.'

'What do you mean?'

'That I must be more careful with him. He seems to get jealous very easily. And, Sandra, don't you think he's fabulous? I honestly think he's the most thrilling man I've ever met. I'm determined to marry him just as soon as possible. The only drawback is that I'll have to put up with Kim. But she can go to boarding school quite soon, I hope.'

Sandra was thinking over this conversation while she

and Kim were packing.

'I've spoken to you twice, Sandra, and you haven't answered,' Kim complained.

'I'm sorry, Kim, what did you say?'

'I said won't it be fun to see Gary again? I do wonder how all those photographs turned out. I guess he'll have printed them by now.'

'What photographs?' asked Sandra, thinking she meant those that Gary had taken of the fishing boats.

Kim put her hands in front of her mouth and opened her grey eyes wide.

'Ooh, I forgot. He said not to tell anyone until he had got them ready. It was to be a nice surprise for people. But he wouldn't mind my telling you, would he? After all, you are his girl-friend.'

Sandra sighed. Really, sometimes Kim could be most exasperating. For no perceptible reason, she had a sudden feeling of dismay.

'What are these photographs, Kim?' she persisted.

'Fabulous ones of the house and me. He said it would be a glorious surprise for Craig.'

'When did he take them?'

'One afternoon when you weren't there. He called for you and then said since he'd missed you would I mind showing him over the house because he had never seen it. And he said would I like him to take some photographs of me to give Craig.'

Sandra was more appalled than surprised. Gary was a newspaper man and anxious to get a scoop. He did not have an ordinary person's fine scruples. Obviously he intended to write the article he had been trying to get for so long about Craig's private life. He could not see any objection to printing it, for of course it would hardly be libellous and would be of great interest.

Sandra thought briefly of phoning him, but it would be difficult to get him from the small village and would only delay their return.

She would speak to him as soon as they were back. That would be in a few hours' time and perhaps it would not be too late to stop him from printing the article. Maybe she was suspecting the worst. Maybe he intended to show it to Craig first. But no, she did not think so.

The return journey was not the happy affair that the outward one had been. Sandra was secretly worrying about Gary and his possible article and she hardly spoke. It was left to Julie to do all the talking, but she kept up a vivacious stream of chatter. Manoel responded gaily to this, but Craig was a little silent, staring ahead at the road as if he had to concentrate on his driving.

A Sunday torpor seemed to envelop the small hotel when Sandra had been left at the entrance and she felt flat and depressed as she went to her room to unpack her suitcase. What had she expected of the weekend? It was foolish to feel in some strange way disappointed. You know that Craig is very much interested in Julie, she admonished herself, so why feel that something is missing? It would have been more than foolish to give him any encouragement last night, and yet. . . .

'Oh, there you are, dear. Home nice and early. Did you have a good time? I'm just going to see to the tea. I've been having a nice nap. I didn't even get around to reading the Sunday papers, but I saw Craig had a write-up in one. I must read it when I have time. The pictures are pretty good.'

Sandra felt a cold chill as she took it from her. It was worse than she had thought. Not only were there pictures of the house and of Kim splashed all over the middle page of the country's most widely read newspaper, but it was joined to a news item about the possibility of a shark attack on this coast and the fact that the Zambesi sharks had been spotted just lately. 'Shark scare threatens five-star hotel owner,' proclaimed the headlines. 'Tycoon loved by lots of beautiful girls, says his daughter.'

'How could he?' whispered Sandra. 'Where's Gary?' she demanded of Aunt Vi. She must have it out with him.

'He's gone to Johannesburg. He's got an interview with one of the big newspapers there. He was very excited about it, and said I was to give you his love.'

So that was that. Having done the damage, he had slipped away. Yet Sandra thought it was hardly fair to blame him too much. He wanted so badly to become well-known in his work. She supposed he thought anything to achieve this object was quite legitimate.

Sandra tried to tell herself that after all what Gary had done was no concern of hers, but every time the phone rang she was sure it would be Craig to question her about the article written by the man he thought was her boy-friend. When at last he phoned it was almost a relief, especially as it was Vi who answered and took a message that Sandra should meet him at the ski boat base as soon as possible. Obviously Vi thought Sandra would be thrilled by this and did not suspect that the interview would be anything but romantic.

This was the first time Sandra had been to the beach since they had come back from their trip and she was surprised to see that near the bathing beach a tall shelter with a ladder had been erected. Two lifesavers were sitting there scanning the sea with binoculars and Craig was talking earnestly to one of them.

'Has anyone seen a shark?' he asked as Sandra drew near.

'I haven't met anyone who's seen one close in to the beach,' the lifesaver said. 'Of course there's always the odd one you see when you go deep-sea fishing. But if you ask me all this talk about the shark menace is just cooked up.'

'But it can do as much damage to a resort like this as if it were true,' said Craig, a frown creasing his brow.

'This was a bright idea of yours to erect this lookout, Mr. Ransom.'

'Yes, except that the sight of it might easily arouse despondency and doubt. However, we must take some precautions. It's no use taking any risks. At the first sight of a fin you must raise the alarm, that is, sound the siren and get everyone out of the water.'

He turned to Sandra, his face sombre.

'Well, Sandra, what do you think of all this?'

'You mean the shark scare?'

'That and other things.'

His grey eyes were hard as steel as he looked down at her. The charming, smiling man of the past weekend had gone, it seemed, beyond recall.

'From my knowledge of you, Sandra, I would have said you were honest as the day. You must be very much in love with this young man of yours to stoop to such a devious way of making it possible for him to write this article.'

Sandra remained silent. What was there to say?

'I must admit I was stunned when this article was brought to my attention. Rather than have my private life dragged all over the newspapers, in such a cheap way and at the expense of my daughter, I would have consented to an interview if it had promised a little more dignity.'

'I'm truly sorry, Craig,' Sandra managed to stammer out. 'Please believe me when I say that I never intended this should happen.'

Craig hardly seemed to hear her.

'It's incredible that you should have allowed Gary to see the house when I thought I'd made it clear that I didn't want it. I thought I was paying you an adequate amount for teaching Kim. You must be very much in need of money, and I surmise you are, but I didn't think you would stoop to conniving at something you knew I didn't want for Kim. Gary must have promised you a substantial cut from his fee.'

Sandra felt as if she had been slapped.

'I can see you don't believe me. But I assure you I did *not* know what Gary's intentions were. I wasn't there when he was shown over the house, otherwise I would have tried to stop it.'

'I wonder. It seems to me that it was you who were instrumental in introducing Kim to Gary. And as for this other thing, the shark scare, your boy-friend has had a hand in publicizing that. I hope he's satisfied now. Remember, it will not only be my hotel that gets the cancellations. Yours will suffer too.'

'I know it,' said Sandra. She could have added that it was going to be the last straw as far as their stringent finances were concerned.

'We'll have to hope that this storm can be weathered. I should have thought that Gary would have more consideration for you at least. Or does he consider that all's fair in the news world even if it comes to spoiling other people's livelihoods?'

'He's young,' said Sandra defensively. 'He wants to

get ahead and he probably didn't realize what damage his report could do. He was only thinking of its news value. I'm sure that when you were his age, Craig, you had few scruples about other people if it came to furthering your ambitions.'

'You must be very much in love with him to make such excuses for his conduct,' said Craig, and turning away from her, as if he could no longer tolerate the sight of her, he strode rapidly along the beach. She was left feeling completely miserable. She wished sincerely that she had never ever met or heard of Craig Ransom, for everything seemed to have gone wrong with her life since he came into it.

The next week was a gloomy one for herself and Vi. By the next post the cancellations started coming in and a note was delivered from Craig saying that he did not want Sandra to give Kim any more lessons. It seemed a pity that the child should suffer for their disagreement and she would miss her, for she had grown fond of Kim. She saw her occasionally at a distance, a lonely little figure, but she had evidently been forbidden to speak to her, since she turned aside when she caught sight of Sandra.

Sandra heard indirectly that the large hotel was also suffering because of the shark rumours. There had been many cancellations of bookings and even the weekend visitors had decreased since it was not so gay with the crowd of holiday people missing.

Then one morning just as Sandra was feeling particularly depressed, Manoel arrived to see them. In his velvet jacket and ruffled cravat he looked strangely out of place in the rustic surroundings of Wave Crest. He glanced around rather scornfully, but Vi was completely oblivious of this. She was surprised but interested that he had come to see them, and disappointed but by no means disconcerted when he refused her offer of home-made lemonade. The nice thing about Vi, Sandra always thought, was that she valued everyone she met as an interesting person and somehow this had the effect of bringing out their best qualities. But this hardly seemed to work with Manoel. He came straight to the point.

'I'm glad to find this opportunity of speaking to you and your aunt, Miss Hamilton. Mr. Ransom has decided that the only thing to do to combat this shark scare is to install nets.'

'But won't that be very expensive?' asked Sandra.

'It will be expensive, of course. But the idea is that as it's in the interests of all hotel owners here, they should all contribute, though naturally Mr. Ransom will put up the major portion of the funds. You'll get off comparatively lightly. What do you say to two thousand rand? That isn't a large sum for a hotel owner, is it?'

Two thousand rand!

'I can never understand this new money, dear.'

'It's over a thousand pounds, Aunt Vi.'

'Oh,' said Vi. 'Oh, dear. Well, I suppose we must try somehow to find it. After all, Craig can hardly be expected to provide protection by himself. We're all in this together.'

It was Sandra who understood the present financial position of the hotel. For a long time she had kept it from Vi just how bad things were, although of course she knew they were struggling to keep things going. But two thousand rand! Where on earth were they to find it? How could Craig possibly think they could afford it? She felt a wave of indignation against him. He must know better than most how impossible it would be.

'I'll go to see the bank manager tomorrow,' she promised. 'Certainly we'll have to join in this scheme.'

'I'm glad you see it this way,' said Manoel, smiling, though very insincerely. 'It's the only way to get the visitors back.'

It might be, thought Sandra, but if we have to borrow another thousand pounds and have as bad a season as we had this year we'll go under.

It was just as she had thought. She had known him for most of her life, but the bank manager was firm, though regretful.

'It's most unfortunate that this story should have arisen at this particular time, Sandra. I had hoped you would weather this bad patch you're going through, but I simply can't take the risk. Your books show a loss, as you know, and I can't lend any more in the fragile hope of things getting better. I'm sorry, but there it is. This big hotel has affected all the small family places. If I lent money to all of them the bank would have to close down itself.'

So that was that. She would have to tell Manoel they could not raise the money. How she wished she could have dealt with Craig himself!

She was walking down the main street not even looking at anyone because she was so deep in thought when she heard the patter of dancing feet behind her and there was Julie, looking as if she did not have a care in the world. Her dark hair was looped up stylishly and she was wearing a two-piece sun-suit in plum-coloured linen.

'Sandra! Just the person I wanted to see. Such exciting news! The shops and big firms here have arranged to have an affair at the hotel to counteract all this bad publicity that your wretched Gary put out.'

Sandra thought ruefully that up to a few weeks ago the wretched Gary had been Julie's, not hers.

'There's to be a smorgasbord lunch by the pool and a beauty contest with big prizes. There's a fashion show too, so the firms will get more trade. The winner of the beauty contest gets a new car or two thousand rand. Mum's dead keen I should enter, but I'm lazy about dieting and I've gained so much weight lately. I'd hate to have to go on a crash course. Come and have some coffee so we can talk.'

Sandra allowed herself to be persuaded to sit down in the middle of the new shopping centre where there were chairs and tables under coloured umbrellas in the open air. Julie gaily greeted all her friends and helped herself from the trolley to a luscious strawberry tart topped with whipped cream. She did not seem to be worrying too much about the proposed dieting. But Sandra felt too discouraged to eat. How were they to manage if she could not raise the money?

'I might not go in for the contest after all,' Julie interrupted her gloomy thoughts. 'Although it's Craig's hotel that's running it, he doesn't seem to approve of that kind of thing, at least not where his girl-friend is involved. Manoel is really the guiding light behind the idea. He's quite bright about organizing functions of this kind and they're all keen to raise funds for the shark nets.'

'But how can they raise funds if they give such a big prize?'

'It's a sprat to catch a mackerel, I suppose. The firms are ones with nation wide interests and they are all contributing. They're going to charge a large amount for the tickets and it's going to be a very fashionable event. There's a ball too a few days later to choose the winner and present the prize.'

When she arrived back at the hotel, the first thing she saw was Gary's recumbent form, clad only in a brief bathing suit. She felt in her present mood that he was the last person she wished to see, but he sprang up from the grass quite unabashed and even gave her an emphatic kiss before she could protest. She looked at him with accusing eyes.

'Yes, I know all about it. I know what a bad chap I've been – Aunt Vi has told me in no uncertain terms. But, ducky, I've landed the most fabulous job, all on account of your snooty boy-friend. And that article won't do him the slightest bit of harm. In fact it will do him good.'

'I don't see how you can believe that. What about the report about the sharks?'

'I hope you don't think I was responsible for that? No, Sandra, I wouldn't have done that to you. It was just unfortunate that someone sent in that report and they splashed it with my article.'

For some reason now that Sandra knew Gary had not been responsible for spreading the shark rumour she felt much better about the whole thing. But she was not going to let him off lightly.

'I thought you acted very irresponsibly anyway. The damage is done now and we have to pay for it.'

'Literally, darling?'

'Yes, I'm afraid so.' She explained about the expense of the shark nets.

'I must put my agile mind to work on this. Leave it to Uncle Gary. Never fear, I'll come up with something.'

Sandra did not really believe him, but that evening

when she was trying to work out the next week's expenses he came to her.

'The beauty contest. That's the solution, darling.'

'Whatever do you mean? It may be a solution for Craig and Manoel, but not for us.'

'I mean you must enter for it. You simply have to win it, dearie, then all your money problems are over, if only for the time being.'

'Don't be ridiculous, Gary. How could I possibly hope to win it?'

'You're too modest, Sandra. You're beautiful in a restrained way. All we have to do is to do you up to look less ladylike and you'll knock them cold.'

'But I'm me. I could never look any different.'

'Oh, yes, you could. You'd be surprised.'

'No, it's impossible.'

'Leave it to me. One of the requirements is to send in photographs, head and shoulders and different poses in a swimsuit so that they can eliminate the non-starters.'

'And one of them will be me.'

'Oh, no, it won't be when I've had a hand in the photography. I could make anyone look sexy.'

'I don't know whether I. . . .'

'Now come on, Sandra, forget about being shy. Think what's at stake. The solution of all your problems, and it won't cost you a bean, I promise you. I've had a large advance on a series of articles I've been commissioned to write and I feel I owe it to you to do something. I'm not taking any refusal. We'll go in to town tomorrow. I have a friend who's a beautician and we'll ask her advice. It won't take much to make you a raving beauty, I'm sure of it.'

'Raving, maybe,' said Sandra, ruefully. 'Beauty . . . I don't know.'

'For God's sake, girl,' said Gary, sounding exasperated, 'hasn't anyone ever told you you could look gorgeous?'

'No,' said Sandra, somewhat startled.

'Come to think of it, you have just the kind of face and figure to get in Playboy Magazine. Maybe we'll have a go at that some day.'

'Gary, for heaven's sake!'

'I'm sure of it. A kind of girl-next-door look combined with an innocent sexiness, slim legs and figure but with the curves in the right places.'

'Manoel didn't think that when I applied for a job at the hotel.'

'Manoel only sees what's obvious. You wait and see.'

True to his promise, the next day Gary arranged an appointment in town with his friend. Sandra had told Vi what they proposed to do and she agreed to hold the fort at the hotel until she returned. Vi was thrilled and delighted and of course completely convinced that Sandra would win the contest. In fact she was rather puzzled that Sandra needed to go to a beautician at all.

'Please promise me not to breathe a word of this,' Sandra implored. 'I would feel such a fool if people started to talk about me.'

'Of course I won't. Cross my heart,' said Vi, making a gesture like an aged Girl Guide. 'You look so lovely in your new dress,' she added. 'It was a good choice.'

Sandra was wearing the new cream dress for her trip in to town since she was determined not to look like a poor relation even if Gary was playing fairy godmother. Her honey-coloured hair was brushed back in to a becoming twist and she was conscious that she looked more attractive than usual. She felt glad of this when, having stopped to open the gate that led from the forest road on to the main highway, she realized that a car that had stopped but was going in the other direction had as its passengers Craig and Kim.

Craig raised his hand in a gesture of greeting, but his expression was cold and he did not speak. Kim, however, called, 'Sandra! Oh, you do look pretty. Where are you going in that new dress?'

'It's a secret, Kim, but we'll tell you soon,' Gary responded.

'How exciting, but I think I can guess.'

'What did she mean by that?' asked Gary. 'How could she possibly guess?'

'She probably thinks we're going in to town to a show,' said Sandra.

She was saddened by this glimpse of Kim and realized how much she had missed the child. Still, it was no use reproaching Gary for this. It was Craig's fault for being so difficult.

Gary's beautician friend regarded Sandra very critically.

'You don't do much to improve yourself, do you, dear?' she said, making Sandra very conscious of her sun-streaked hair and her lack of make-up. Charleen had certainly worked to achieve her own type of looks, with her crown of Titian curls, her black artificial lashes and the dead white skin emphasized by the scarlet lips.

'Don't try to make her look like you, for God's sake, Charleen,' Gary said frankly.

'That would be difficult,' Charleen said a bit smugly, not understanding any slight in Gary's words. 'I see Sandra as the natural type. It's a bit difficult to make her look like a beauty contest winner.'

'I couldn't agree more,' said Sandra. 'You see, Gary, it's a mad idea.'

'Don't be so hasty. I'm sure that Charleen, given time, can achieve wonders.'

'I tell you what I'll do,' said Charleen, responding to Gary's flattery. 'I'll do a light make-up today for the photographs and this will give me some idea of Sandra's possibilities. Then I'll come out on the morning of the contest and give her a good going over. In the meantime I'll think it over. Don't worry, ducky. If anyone can make you look gorgeous, it's me.'

Sandra had grave misgivings after this interview. She would look quite ludicrous if she was made up in the fashion Charleen seemed to favour. And when Gary insisted on accompanying her to buy a swimsuit for the contest, she came near to open rebellion.

'I want a costume at once provocative and yet at the same time virginal,' he said to the somewhat bewildered saleslady.

'We have some new ones in from Paris,' she said. 'Perhaps we can find something suitable amongst those.'

They were beautiful, Sandra had to admit.

'But I can't show so much of me,' she protested as she tried a white lacy one very low cut at the bosom and equally high cut to reveal her beautiful legs to the best advantage.

'You look quite gorgeous,' enthused the saleslady, but Sandra felt she would never have the courage to wear such a costume in public. She said as much to Gary.

'Forget it, darling. You look lovely. It gives just the effect I wanted. Please wear it, for Uncle Gary's sake.

Think of all those lovely yards of shark-netting!'

Sandra admitted to herself that she must be practical about it. If she was going in for this contest she must do it wholeheartedly. But wasn't the whole thing crazy anyway?

Gary had borrowed a friend's studio in town and he spent a long time posing Sandra to take the required photographs.

'Think of someone you love,' he admonished her when he was taking close-ups. 'No, not like that. I don't mean you should think of your maiden aunt, nice as she is.'

The shadowy face of Craig came unsought, the tender expression he had worn on those occasions that were so very few.

'Beautiful ... just right. I didn't know your lips could look like that!' Gary exulted. 'That one will be a winner.'

By the time they arrived back at Wave Crest, Sandra was exhausted.

'I don't call it very clever to make you look like that,' Vi protested. 'Why, you're quite washed out. Go and sit down and I'll bring you a cup of beef tea.'

When she had brought it she sat down to chat.

'I had quite an exciting time while you were out,' she announced. 'Craig and Kim came to call.'

Sandra thought with a stab at the heart that Craig had seized the opportunity, knowing that she was out.

'He was very pleasant and Kim says she misses her lessons but that Craig said it was too much trouble for you. She's a funny wee girl, isn't she? Do you know what she said? That Gary said you were going in to town for something secret and she was sure he meant you were going to buy an engagement ring. Wasn't that quaint? She was so set on the idea I hadn't the heart to tell her she was wrong. She'll find out soon enough, I guess.'

'Did Craig hear her say that?' asked Sandra.

'Yes, but he didn't say anything. It won't do him any harm to think you have someone else in tow.'

Sandra felt too tired to work all this out or to deny to Vi that Craig had any interest in her. Like Kim, she would find out soon enough that she was wrong.

CHAPTER NINE

SANDRA woke early in the small round hut that had been her home for almost as long as she could remember. Sunlight fell in bars across the plain white coverlet and she reflected that since she had met Craig winter had gone and the swift African spring had taken its place.

Birds were calling from the trees in clear vibrant notes and a green creeper tapped its new leaves against the windowsill. So why did she feel this flat depressed sense of doom this morning? Of course. It was the day of the beauty contest. I must have been mad, she thought. It's impossible for me to go through with it. How could I have let Gary persuade me? Her whole being cringed away from the idea of the ordeal she would have to undergo this afternoon and she thought briefly of cancelling her entry. The very idea that I could win is ridiculous, she thought.

But Gary had gone to so much trouble and she felt reluctant to let him down. And Vi was so keen she should enter. But she knew she could not win, especially when she thought of the time when she had tried to get the job at the hotel. All the girls had been so much more attractive than she was and so much more confident too. And this would be even worse. She thought too of Craig and Julie. Julie had said Craig disapproved of the competition, but she was still determined to enter for it. What chance did she, Sandra, stand against Julie?

Fortunately she was kept very busy during the early

part of the morning and gradually her spirits lifted a little. In the middle of the morning, Charleen arrived, and the rest of the time was occupied with the rites of her trade. She was as good as her word. She gave Sandra a shining colour rinse that emphasized the honey-gold of her hair and it was set in a curving swirl that bounced on her shoulders. She was given a subtle make-up, her eyes emphasized by soft shadows and enlarged by eyeliner. Her naturally dark lashes had another set added to them so that her brown eyes looked huge and luminous. Her golden tan was beautifully even from her long hours with Kim in the mild winter sun, but where the brief costume revealed more skin than usual Charleen shaded the hard line so that the difference looked infinitely alluring.

Charleen worked like an artist concentrating on a masterpiece, and by the time she had finished, Sandra could scarcely recognize the willowy beauty who faced her in the mirror. She had decided not to go to the smorgasbord lunch since Gary had insisted that she must only appear for the contest, for he wanted to introduce an element of surprise.

But when she walked into the dressing-room shortly before the contest, the first person she saw was Julie. At any other time the astonishment registered on her face would have amused Sandra.

'Sandra, what have you done to yourself? I scarcely recognized you. You're not. . . . You don't mean to say you're entering for the contest!'

'I had thought of it,' smiled Sandra.

Somehow Julie's reaction had given her courage, together with the knowledge of what the mirror had told her.

'But you can't! I mean how can you? It isn't your

thing at all. You've never shown any interest in anything like this before.'

And I won't again, thought Sandra.

'Gary thought I might as well have a try. He sent my photographs in,' she admitted.

'Gary? I might have known it. Well, I hope you won't regret it, Sandra. After all, you aren't used to parading in front of a crowd. Look how shy you were when you went for that interview.'

It was rather mean of Julie to bring that up, thought Sandra. She knew she looked more beautiful than she had ever looked before, thanks to Charleen's efforts, but within her there was still the same shy girl shrinking away from the thought of exhibiting herself in public.

She was glad when they heard the announcer calling for the contestants. It would soon be over, thank goodness. She could not possibly get beyond the first round and then she could go back to being ordinary workaday Sandra. The other girls in the dressing-room were all strangers to her, but they looked at her with critical eyes when she discarded her wrap.

'I'd be ashamed to wear a costume that was so revealing,' she heard one girl say to another.

'Some people will do anything to look sexy,' the other one agreed.

'What did Aunt Vi think of your swimsuit?' asked Julie maliciously.

'She hasn't seen it,' Sandra admitted.

'I suppose Gary chose it for you. He couldn't care what people say about you so long as he gets daring pictures for his paper.'

I won't let them affect me, thought Sandra, but her spirits drooped and she wished she had never entered for the wretched contest. But it was now too late. As if in a dream, Sandra walked out in to the sunlight beside the pool. A huge number of people had gathered around the ramp that stretched, it seemed to her fevered imagination, at least five miles in front of her.

As each girl paraded there was a murmur from the vast crowd and comments about their face and figure were clearly audible. Now that Sandra had launched herself into this she was determined to try to do Gary's efforts justice and she walked gracefully, smiling around her. But although she did not relish the idea of hearing comments about her appearance, she felt slightly worried that people seemed to be quieter when she appeared than they were for the other girls.

She was sure that this must be a sign that they did not think her up to beauty contest standard and she tried hard to emulate the swaying gait of her fellow contestants, but it was hopeless. In spite of her improved and glamorous appearance, she still felt that she was very ordinary compared with the rest.

At least, though, she seemed to be blessed with as much intelligence as anyone else. The questions they asked were easy to answer and her low clear voice carried well over the microphone, but she was very glad when the ordeal was over and she was free to sit down while the judges conferred. Julie obviously knew none of Sandra's qualms. She was full of confidence, although she did not do too well during the spoken interview. It was true, thought Sandra, that she had gained considerably in weight lately since she had worked at the hotel, but her dark pouting beauty was like that of a flamboyant tropical flower just at the height of its loveliness before the petals begin to fall.

Alas, the ordeal was not over yet. Sandra was asked

to come forward with Julie and a few other girls. Well, it seemed she had not been eliminated in the first round. Again she had to endure the sensation of being gazed upon by a few hundred people, but this time she seemed to be getting used to it and was more at ease. She even managed to laugh at one of the judges' quips, but she would be glad when it was all over.

There were more consultations and, while this was going on, Sandra felt free to look around. Before this she had only been aware of a seething mass of white blobs, the way the crowd appeared to her nervous imagination, but now she was able to distinguish faces and she looked around to see if she could recognize anyone.

There was Vi, in the front row, and not looking in the least disapproving of her abbreviated swimsuit, smiling and giving a surreptitious wave, her silky grey hair all disordered in the slight sea breeze.

How could she have thought she would disapprove when everything Sandra did always seemed perfect to her? And there was Gary, his red hair ruffled wildly, his freckled face one big beam from ear to ear as he clasped his fists and waved her an encouraging sign. And Kim was there. She had somehow wormed her way to sit in front of the spectators' chairs and she was utterly absorbed in looking at Sandra with admiring devotion. Well, thought Sandra, if Vi and Kim were judges I might stand a chance.

And, as she was thinking this, she was suddenly aware that someone else was looking at her with anything but admiration. Craig's tall figure overtopped the spectators who were standing behind the chairs and even from this distance she could sense his disapproval. She felt as if she was alone with him and trying to countenance that burning gaze that must surely shrivel all her attempts to be calm. Suddenly she was hideously aware that she was standing in front of hundreds of people in a swimsuit designed to show as much as possible of her slim young body, and that every artifice had been used to improve her natural appearance. Yet at the same time that she felt shamed by Craig's bitter stare she also felt indignant that he could make her feel like this. What right had he to give her that critical regard? What did he know of her reasons for subjecting herself to this ordeal?

But now there was a flurry and a stir amongst the spectators, for the judges had come forward with a fanfare from the orchestra and were obviously about to announce the names of the six finalists. Sandra was amazed to hear her name.

She felt a glow of surprised joy, followed swiftly by a feeling of apprehension. So the ordeal was not yet over. She would have to face up to appearing in public again at the ball some days later. But she was so surprised that she had been chosen as one of the finalists.

'But I thought . . .' she stammered to Gary some time later . . . 'I thought they didn't like me.'

'They liked you all right.' Gary's red hair stood on end in his exuberance at the success of his plan so far.

'But they didn't make remarks like they did when the other girls went past. They were all so quiet.'

'Dumbstruck, my dear. What did I tell you? Just struck dumb by your beautiful, ladylike glamour.'

For the first time since her ordeal began, Sandra laughed. Really, Gary was incorrigible!

'I haven't won it yet,' she pointed out. 'Nor do I expect to.'

'What about a spot of positive thinking, Sandra?'

urged Gary. 'Friend Craig doesn't waste any time latching on to Julie,' he added rather bitterly. Sandra glanced up. Julie was talking in a very animated fashion to Craig and he was smiling down in to her eyes, seemingly oblivious of the fact that he had previously expressed his disapproval of Julie's entering the contest.

Julie saw them and beckoned.

'Sandra, dear, what a lovely surprise for you! Doesn't she look wonderful, Craig? Isn't it amazing what proper make-up can do?'

But Craig did not reply. His dark gaze coldly seemed to take in the fact that Gary had his arm around Sandra's bare waist.

'I must go to find my wrap,' she said hastily, and went towards the dressing-rooms. The rest of the girls had gone and she sat there for a long time, tired after her ordeal and strangely depressed in spite of the fact that she had done so well in the contest.

When she came out again Gary was nowhere to be seen. She had refused his offer to join him in a drink, for she wanted to get back to Vi. She set off along the beach in the direction of their hotel. How quiet it was! Almost deserted. Everyone was up at the hotel having drinks or preparing for the evening meal. There was only one late swimmer far out in the waves that were gilded now by the light of the setting sun.

It was still warm and Sandra was seized by a desire to plunge into the golden waves and wash away all the sordidness of her afternoon's ordeal. What did it matter that Gary's precious costume was meant only for display? As far as she was concerned she never wanted to wear it again. Thank goodness she had to appear in an evening dress at the ball.

She ran into the water, rushing into the first breaking wave as if to cast herself into the sea's wild embrace, heedless of the careful make-up and hairdo that had cost Charleen such pains. The lonely swimmer was nearer now, the last rays of the sun glinting gold upon his dark hair. With a shock Sandra realized his identity and at almost the same instant Craig came coasting in upon a wave directly towards her.

She turned and tried to get away, swiftly cleaving the burnished waves with her strongest swimming style, but Craig was faster and seemed equally determined that he should catch up with her. She felt herself seized by the shoulders and felt a strong inclination to struggle like a person who was drowning. He was laughing at her feeble attempts to escape his grasp and she ceased to fight against him but let herself be drawn relentlessly towards the shore, where they stood at last facing each other like two statues bronzed by the low rays of the setting sun.

'You surprise me, Sandra,' he said at last. 'But that's not unusual, is it?'

'What do you mean, Craig?'

'I would have thought you would be celebrating your win in a more suitable fashion than this. You seem at the moment to be singularly lacking in vanity if you can plunge into the sea and ruin your hairdo, wash away all your make-up and risk spoiling that very exiguous costume.'

The expression that had been like a stone mask had vanished and now his eyes were sparkling with wicked amusement.

'You surprise me too, Craig,' she declared before she had time to consider her words. 'When I'd been made to look beautiful, you looked at me as if I were some kind of distasteful object that had drifted on to the beach, but now that all the gorgeous glamour has gone I seem to amuse you.'

'Did you call that get-up gorgeous? Really, Sandra, I was never more appalled than when I saw you making a show of yourself for that gaping crowd. Why on earth did you do it?'

She was determined not to reveal to him that she had done it for money. He had thought her grasping enough over Gary's article with even less foundation.

'Why shouldn't I have done it?' she asked. 'What does your opinion matter to me? Other people must have thought I looked good. Every girl has a secret dream of being judged beautiful. Even in fairy stories you have the theme. Don't you remember? "Mirror, mirror on the wall, who is fairest of them all?"'

'But you, Sandra . . . I would have said you would be the last girl in the world to put yourself on show. I've always found you most reticent in every way.'

Sandra laughed. 'But then you hardly know me, do you, Craig? Because I've rebuffed you once or twice, you seem to have the impression that I'm shy. I may not be like that to everyone, you know.'

'It does seem I had the wrong impression. Let's say I've never understood you.'

'There's no necessity that you should, is there, Craig?'

'No, I admit that. But if I had any influence on you at all I would beg you to give up this contest. Really, Sandra, self-display is not for you.'

'Why should you have any influence?'

Craig's face hardened. 'Why indeed?'

As he strode away down the beach, she had a stupid

desire to run after him and to use any means in her power to relax the obstinate set of that dark head, and to see again the teasing mischievous smile that, however infuriating, was infinitely preferable to the cold dark anger. But, shocked by the strength of her own feelings, she turned swiftly and walked slowly away in the direction of the little hotel.

CHAPTER TEN

Two days later as Gary drove his beach buggy along the crowded esplanade of the neighbouring seaside town, Sandra tried to feel as elated as he obviously expected her to be and failed dismally.

The sun was sparkling on distant waves and the whole scene was one of ease, gaiety and good living. The hotels along the sea-front had been newly painted for the season and the bright lighting arrangements refurbished. Crowds of young people clad in bikinis and sometimes carrying surfboards crossed at the traffic lights to find their way to the beach. On the sea ships rode at anchor waiting to come into harbour.

'It's no time to be stingy at this stage,' Gary had answered when she had protested at his declared intention to take her in to buy a new evening dress. 'You're my masterpiece. Please give me the pleasure of gilding the lily.'

As she had come to expect, Gary's ideas on what she should wear to the ball were highly original.

'We've used the all-revealing lark,' he said, 'and you must admit it paid off handsomely, but now's the time to look splendidly lovely in some gorgeous exotic get-up. How about that?'

'You know I could never ... oh, well. ...' Sandra replied a little feebly. She knew there was no stopping Gary when he was on to what he thought was a bright idea.

'We'll go to the Indian quarter,' Gary announced. 'Indian clothes are the most gorgeous, modest yet provocative garb one can get. You aren't dark, but we'll go for one of those glowing colours that will knock their eyes out.'

In this modern coastal city of Southern Africa, it was amazing to find a neighbourhood quite close to the central streets of huge department stores that could almost have been taken for a part of Bombay. There were mosques with gilded domes shining in the brilliant sunlight, and there were food shops spilling out their wares on to the pavements in sacks of red chillies, cloves of garlic, and heavily fragrant spices. The names above the shop fronts were strange and foreign, but most of the families of these Indians had been in South Africa for more than a hundred years. They had kept their own culture and in the streets the slender dark young women looked flowerlike and graceful in saris made of filmy material.

'This is the place,' said Gary, and they entered a shop with display windows full of brilliant exciting-looking garments. The Indian girl who came forward to help them was fragile as dandelion silk. Gold ear-rings studded with rubies swung from her small ears and her black hair fell smoothly into a graceful knot. Sandra, in spite of her own slenderness, felt quite clumsy beside her, but the girl was very helpful and most interested in finding a suitably glamorous garment that Sandra could wear to the ball.

There was a very wide choice of lovely unusual clothes. Sandra was tempted by the batik-patterned two-piece dresses known as lungis, the skirt manipulated in folds like a sari and the top loose-fitting and graceful. But there were kaftans as well, loose long silk robes with all the colours of the paintbox splashed across the mat-erial. However, Gary was adamant that he wanted to see Sandra in a sari and when one was produced in a rich amber colour, brilliantly decorated with gold thread, he declared that it was exactly what he wanted her to wear. The Indian girl said too that it suited her and that she walked 'much more gracefully than most European ladies.'

Sandra herself was pleasantly surprised by her reflection in the long mirror. The rich amber colour brought out the gilt lights of her hair and seemed to emphasize the pansy brown in her eyes. A tight-fitting top revealed the golden skin of her back and midriff. Gary was right. The sari was clinging and provocative yet at the same time modest and utterly glamorous. The Indian girl taught her how to drape the yards of filmy material leaving a long piece to cover the bodice and hang in lovely folds. A pair of gold Indian sandals were produced, their small toe-straps sequin-covered.

Not to be outdone, Gary bought himself a long embroidered shirt in brilliant purple that contrasted wildly with his bright red hair. He insisted that he must wear it straight away. Sandra had booked a table for lunch at one of the older and more dignified hotels where she hoped the aged residents would not be interested in seeing a beauty contestant, but she had reckoned without Gary's flamboyance. They would scarcely be inconspicuous when he appeared in that shirt, she thought. She herself had succumbed to the temptation of buying one of the cotton batik tunics and Gary insisted that she should wear it. Worn as a dress it was a little short, but her long brown legs looked very beautiful, Gary assured her.

The interest and gaiety of the shopping expedition had certainly raised her spirits and she was laughing at some joke of Gary's when they entered the palm-decorated quadrangle of the hotel, the place where people sat in the open to have their aperitifs before going in to lunch.

'Don't look now,' said Gary, as he ordered a beer for himself and apple juice for Sandra, 'but your friend is here. Entertaining a lovely lady, but it looks like he has competition.'

Sandra did not pretend not to know it was Craig that Gary had seen. It was too infuriating the way her heart beat quicker whenever she became aware of his presence. At the first opportunity she ventured a glance in the direction Gary had indicated. Yes, there he was. 'A pirate in a business suit', Julie had once called him, and he looked astonishingly handsome in a dark formal suit, light striped shirt and Dior tie, yet still a little rakish.

'But that's Louise and her husband John Tremayne,' she exclaimed as she took in the appearance of Craig's companions. 'We were at school together, but I haven't seen her for ages. She married John straight from school. He's a sugar farmer from the north coast and I believe they have a fabulous seaside place too.'

At almost the same time Louise looked over in their direction and waved her hand, making some remark to Craig and smiling vivaciously. She was a lovely blonde who hardly looked older than she had at school, although she was now the mother of two children. In a little while, excusing herself from Craig and her husband, she came hurrying over to their table.

'Sandra, I'm so pleased to see you. I read all about the beauty contest and I think it's fabulous that you're amongst the finalists. I'll hold thumbs that you win. I was just telling Craig that you were always the one with brains as well as beauty, of course, while poor me had to battle along as best I could.'

Louise did not look as if she was having too poor a time of it now, reflected Sandra. She was wearing an exquisite suit of pale pink linen that must have cost the earth and her soft cream suede shoes with bag to match proclaimed their Parisian origin. But she was still the same charming, vivacious Louise who had befriended the quieter Sandra in their schooldays. Her deep blue eyes sparkled with friendliness and affection as she said now, 'I can't let you go now without a chat. Craig and my husband are having a tiresome business chat, but won't you join us for coffee when you've had lunch?'

Sandra looked at Gary. She was sure he would provide her with some excuse to refuse, although quite truthfully she was torn between the desire to renew her old tie with Louise and her wish not to have to meet Craig again. But Gary nodded, too carried away by Louise's charm to object to having coffee with Craig.

This was one of the city's oldest hotels and its lofty dining-room had been the scene of many gay balls in the past. Beneath its ornate plastered ceiling was a musician's gallery where a former Prince of Wales had once made an appearance. Even the waiters seemed like figures from the past, for they were elderly Indians with white high-necked uniforms and formal red turbans.

The leisurely atmosphere was delightful to Sandra who usually took her lunch in snatches while standing in the kitchen supervising the serving of the meal to their visitors. They ordered soles, grilled golden brown and bordered by prawns and mushrooms.

'This place is all coming down next year, you know,' said Gary as Sandra was admiring the exquisite silver épergne cascading roses and carnations from its stand on a raised dais.

'No!' exclaimed Sandra. She was usually so busy that she did not keep up with the local news.

'Yes, pet, more progress. The building has been declared unsafe because of the increased traffic on the esplanade and it will be too costly to restore it in its present form. They're knocking it down and replacing it with a huge towerlike block many stories high.'

How sad to visualize this dignified building being replaced by another hotel on the lines of the Casa del Sol with its discothèque and cocktail bars.

'Don't look so grief-stricken, Sandra. I never knew such a girl for living in the past! You must admit the place needs a bit of shaking up. Sight all those old dollies eyeing my shirt with icy disapproval. And your legs in that batik tunic are not coming in for very favourable criticism, I'll be bound.'

It was true that the old ladies who constituted the hotel's permanent boarders were looking at Gary and Sandra as if they were not used to the modern way of dressing. But this was nothing to the cold stare that Sandra got from Craig when they met for coffee on the outside balcony, a place bounded by beautiful old wrought iron balustrades that overlooked the bay alive with shipping of all kinds.

But if Louise noticed the air of tension she made light of it. She chatted away to Sandra, leaving the others little chance to talk.

'We must get together again. I'm longing to show off my kidlets to you.' Her blue eyes sparkled. 'Why, I've got the most marvellous idea! Of course you can come with Craig, when he visits us next week.'

Sandra was horrified. 'Oh, no, I couldn't possibly leave the hotel. I've far too much to do, Louise.'

'But it's only for one day, a few hours, in fact. I wish we could have you for longer. Craig is chartering a plane next week and flying to see the land we own on the north coast. He's coming to lunch with us at the sea cottage. And you can come too. Don't you think that's a bright idea?'

Gary intervened, 'But you can't take Sandra away before the contest.'

'It's the day before, but it will do Sandra good to get away from the hotel. It will be quite a restful trip in the plane.'

Sandra stole a doubtful look at Craig. He was frowning. Of course it was the last thing he wanted to do, but what chance had he against Louise's charming determination to get her way?

'I'd love to bring Sandra,' he declared abruptly.

What a barefaced lie, thought Sandra. But she found herself unwillingly inveigled into agreeing with Louise's plans.

'We'll be back in time for dinner,' Craig assured her. 'I'll be glad of company on the flight there and back. And you know the coast well. Maybe you'll be able to give me some practical advice.'

Gary had apparently revised his opinion of the trip too, for on the way back he said, 'Maybe you can supply me with hot news about Craig's future plans.'

Sandra thought regretfully that however little she wished for Craig's company she always seemed to be getting pushed in his direction. On the day planned for the flight, the birds had only just begun to call a few tentatives notes when she started to dress. She decided it would be practical to wear slacks for the journey, but took her pleated skirt to change into in case it was very hot by the time they arrived. The further up the coast they went the hotter it would become.

She went into the kitchen to make sandwiches and coffee and to her own annoyance found that her hands were trembling. She tried hard to quell the nervous excitement she felt at the idea of spending the day with Craig and tried to tell herself it was just the idea of the plane journey that was causing this stupid feeling. With this in mind she took a tablet to guard against travel-sickness. At least she wanted to be spared the humiliation of feeling ill in his presence, for she was sure he had a rock-hard constitution and would have no sympathy for weakness.

She had thought there would be some awkward feeling after the bitter words of their meeting on the beach, but when he drew up his car on the grass in front of the hotel, she felt a sensation that she had hardly expected, a surge of joy at seeing him again and a thrilled feeling that whole day lay in front of her to be shared with Craig. Her doubts vanished when she saw his charming smile. What did it matter that she knew deep in her heart it did not mean anything? And that she doubted that they could get through the day with no argument. At least there was to be a happy beginning.

The small trim aircraft, fuelled and ready to go, was awaiting them at the airport for private planes.

'I didn't know you could pilot a plane,' said Sandra, and felt rather foolish when he turned to her with a grin and said, 'I can do most things, some better than others. Surely you knew that?'

Fortunately there was not much opportunity for conversation when they were in the air. Sandra had never before flown up the coast and at first the landscape was familiar yet strange seen from this height. Blue sea washed its white waves in to curving beaches and little bays bordered by semi-tropical growth, tangled bush and wild banana trees. Inland stretched the sugar cane country with its rolling hills of green luxurious growth, sometimes divided by one-way tracks where small cane trains transported the harvested stems.

Craig pointed out settlements along the coast, collections of little white houses surrounded by small pieces of cultivated land. Gradually, however, the landscape changed and became wilder. Flat-topped trees showed in little groups in a wide expanse of grassland. The great lake on the edge of which they had stayed for that week-end still looked vast from the air, but Sandra could see now how it was cut off from the sea by only a small barrier of sand dunes.

There were signs of civilization again, plantations of gum trees and more sugar cane, and soon they were descending to where a windsock pointed out the existence of a landing ground. John Tremayne, Louise's husband, was waiting for them, ready to drive them the forty odd miles to their holiday home. It was not exactly Sandra's idea of a coast cottage, for, set in the wild bush as it was, it still had every modern luxury. It was rather like a Swiss chalet with an open verandah of wood running the whole length of the upper storey. The bedrooms opened on to this so that they got the maximum fresh air and benefited from the cool breezes that blew from the sea.

Louise came running across the paved patio when she heard the car. Her two children were with her, delightful little girls of two and four years with blonde plaits and blue eyes. They were dressed in diminutive bikini costumes and obviously spent much of their lives in the sun.

'I'm so glad you brought Sandra, Craig. Now we're going to have a lovely long chat while you and John go to look at this tiresome land. I hope you buy it from John. He has far too much land already and it would be most exciting if you built a hotel here as glamorous as your other one. Don't you agree, Sandra?'

Craig laughed, 'Sandra doesn't approve of my building activities, Louise. She thinks I spoil the old order of things.'

'Why ever not, Sandra? If you lived here you'd be all for a bit more life around the place. I love meeting more people. Please do develop this place, Craig. I certainly won't object.'

Watching Craig smiling down at Louise, Sandra thought regretfully how easy it would have been if she had taken this view. There was no stopping all the changes that were taking place and if she had accepted it gratefully instead of always arguing maybe Craig and she would not always have been at loggerheads. But then there was so much more involved, her own and Vi's livelihood and way of life.

A dark soft-footed servant brought tea to them upon the patio overlooking the sea and they ate hot scones dripping with cream and honey. It was so peaceful here. Beyond the tangled screen of wild bushes and banana trees the sea murmured softly down below upon the small private beach. Upon the patio there were white tubs spilling red geraniums and flame-coloured bougainvilleas. A small fountain tinkled, its cascade of clear water dripping from a dolphin's mouth, and on the surrounding walls were ceramics of fishes and sea creatures that had come from Italy, as Louise informed her. She and John had toured Europe on their honeymoon trip.

Craig and John went off to inspect the land and Louise, consigning the children to the beach in the company of their nanny, seized the opportunity to have a real heart-to-heart talk with Sandra.

'What a gorgeous man!' she exclaimed as she watched the two men walking towards the car. 'Almost as exciting as my John. What are you doing about him, Sandra?'

Sandra tried to laugh off her friend's enthusiasm.

'I'm not interested in him, nor he in me, if that's what you mean, Louise.'

'Nonsense. There's something in the air when I see you together. Something electric. You can't tell me you aren't interested, Sandra.'

'You've become a matchmaker since you married, Louise. I assure you we don't even get on well together.'

'That's not necessary at first. Sometimes a bit of conflict is good for an affair.' She nodded her head wisely. 'I know.'

Sandra smiled. It was true she remembered that Louise had been interested in John when she was still at school and she remembered the tears and quarrels and all the varied confidences to which she had had to listen. But Louise had been very young then. How lucky she had been to find her happy niche in life so soon.

'Wasn't he terribly impressed when you entered for the beauty contest and did so well?' Louise demanded.

'He was frightfully disapproving. Not that it had anything to do with him. You're making a story up about something that doesn't even exist.'

'Probably a good sign,' said Louise, brushing this

aside. 'It shows he's jealous of other men noticing you.'

'You're as bad as Vi,' Sandra protested. 'Let's talk about something else. Tell me about your little girls.' And Louise was willingly diverted on to this fascinating subject.

Later they spoke of the difficulties that Sandra was experiencing in running the hotel. It was wonderful to have someone to confide in, a friend of long standing. For such a long time Sandra had kept her troubles to herself, for Julie was never interested. Louise was such a sympathetic listener that Sandra was almost tempted to discuss her own bewilderment at the manner in which she felt herself more and more deeply enmeshed by Craig's dark magnetism, even though he obviously disliked her. But no, she could not speak of that. It was her very close secret.

CHAPTER ELEVEN

THEY had yielded to the temptation of lingering far too long over lunch. Craig and John had arrived back hot and a little weary, so it was decided that a swim would be a good pick-me-up. The water was delightful and it was hard to leave it. Then of course Louise served drinks before lunch and they chatted very happily over their beer and light wine until by the time they sat down to cold chicken and salad it was mid-afternoon. But time did not seem to matter in this delightful place, and John and Louise were obviously so pleased to have their company that it was hard to tear themselves away. How enjoyable the day had been in spite of her forebodings, thought Sandra as she waved good-bye to Louise and the little girls.

'Come again soon, but stay longer,' called Louise. 'And that means both of you!'

When they sat in the plane preparatory to taking off, Sandra realized that this was the first time she had been alone with Craig since this morning. She felt a little drowsy from all the good food and drink but very happy.

'What a lovely day it's been,' she said.

He smiled at her and she was very conscious of the small space of the cockpit in which they seemed to be enclosed with an intimate nearness that cut them off from the ordinary workaday world. There seemed to be no one else in existence but herself and this dark man with the attractive grin and the lean brown hands cautiously handling the controls.

A short run over the turf and they were away. The sun was dipping low over the sea.

'We should have started off an hour ago,' said Craig, 'but I hadn't the heart to tear you away from your old friend.'

Sandra wanted to say that she had not noticed any particular urgency on his part. He had seemed to be enjoying John's company just as well as she had enjoyed Louise's. But she thought it best to keep quiet. They had spent the whole day free of the usual arguments that seemed to arise when they were in each other's company. So she must keep the peace for a little while longer.

The shadows of the sand dunes were falling over the beaches and they looked dark and a little cold now. At this time, unlike the glowing sensation of the morning flight, it seemed a little depressing and sombre. Sandra thought she would be glad to be home, sitting having a sherry with Aunt Vi and telling her about Louise's house and children.

'Won't be long now,' said Craig, as if reading her thoughts.

'I'm not worried that we're late,' Sandra assured him. 'It should be lovely to see the sunset from this height.'

Craig turned to smile at her.

'Sometimes you seem so sweet, Sandra. It's hard to believe that at other times you can be the most aggravating little puss in the world.'

'Well!' said Sandra. 'If that isn't the pot calling the kettle black! How can you call me aggravating when you're the most exasperating man I've ever met?'

He grinned mischievously.

'That's what I like about you, Sandra. You always

come back fighting.'

For a little while they were quiet, but in spite of their previous conversation Sandra had a feeling of something near contentment as they flew high above the coast. She felt herself falling asleep, lulled by the steady drone of the engine and the sense of security that came from being near to Craig.

But she was jerked awake by a nerve-shaking noise, a sudden splutter that came as a harsh shock. The engine had changed its note. There was something in this hitherto smooth-flying sleek machine that was not quite right. The spluttering missing noise was very different from the smooth singing tone she had heard before. It all happened very suddenly. The plane began to lose height.

'Is your safety belt fastened properly, Sandra? I'm afraid there's nothing for it but a forced landing. Don't be too scared. There's plenty of flat beach around here. I'll go for that.'

Craig did not have time to say any more. He was busy sending out messages by radio, trying to convey their position to the nearest airport. And at the same time he was looking out for a place that looked safe for landing.

There was hardly time to feel anything but blank disbelief as Craig brought the plane lower and lower. Trees that had been patches of darker colour in the surrounding landscape now revealed themselves as dangerous leafy tops, but they skimmed past these over the high sand dunes and above the level beach. For a few terrible moments Sandra thought they were going to miss the sand and come down into the sea. She had said not one word since the emergency began. She glanced at Craig. His jaw looked taut, but he took his hands from the controls for a couple of seconds and pressed hers firmly. How could he manage to smile?

'Try to relax,' he said. 'The landing might be a spot bumpy, but we'll be safe, you'll see.'

Somehow she found the courage to smile back at him.

'Of course we'll be all right,' she said, while her mind fought off thoughts of the plane bursting into flames as soon as they hit the ground.

And then they were down, bumping along the sand in a wild dust storm but otherwise unharmed. They were above high water mark when the plane slewed around in the soft sand and refused to go further.

When he had turned the engine off, Craig sat for a moment before turning to look at her.

'We'd better get out of this quickly,' he said. 'I don't think it will catch alight now, but let's go.'

Sandra was surprised to find that her legs were trembling so much that she could not stand. She turned beseechingly to Craig.

'Somehow I don't seem able to. . . .'

She found herself in his arms being firmly helped from the plane and made to walk the distance that Craig considered safe before he made her sit down in the shelter of a grove of banana trees. But he still held on to her and this time she was grateful. It was wonderful to feel safe and sheltered. She allowed herself to be weak-minded for once and to enjoy the strength and comfort of his arms.

'Sandra, my darling, are you all right?'

Had she imagined the endearment? She felt quite lightheaded, certainly.

'I . . . I think so.'

'You were wonderful, so brave, so cool. Most girls

would have had screaming hysterics, but not Sandra. You really are a remarkable person, aren't you?'

Did he think her unfeminine that she had not shown visible fear? If he only knew what had gone on inside her. . . . She smiled suddenly.

'You were pretty cool yourself, Craig.'

He seemed to become conscious that he still had her in his arms and letting go of her abruptly he stood up and looked up and down the beach.

'I must go to see if the radio is still operating. I managed to get one message across before we came down. The plane should be safe enough here for the time being. There's nothing we can do about that, anyway. We'd better walk over the sand dunes and see if we can come across a ranger's cottage.'

He went back to the plane and Sandra was left alone.

The sun was finally setting behind a bank of cloud and Sandra knew that night would come swiftly, for there were no long twilights in this sub-tropical part of Africa. She felt weak and her legs still trembled from the sudden shock of their descent. But what was the alternative to ascending the sand dunes and looking for shelter? It was to stay the night on the beach with Craig. If she had found the intimate atmosphere of the cabin too overwhelming when they were in flight, what would it be like to spend the many hours of the night on this lonely beach with a man who had previously tried to make love to her at every opportunity?

She tried to turn her mind to practical matters. Craig had come back, having succeeded in getting a message through.

'We still have a flask of coffee and some sandwiches in the plane. They might come in useful,' she suggested.

'Coffee with plenty of sugar would be a splendid idea right now.'

It tasted wonderful. They had one cup each and one sandwich, carefully conserving the rest.

'We might need those for breakfast. They can't send help until tomorrow morning,' said Craig. 'I'll go and have a look over the dunes if you don't mind staying here for a while.'

Sandra shivered. 'Don't leave me, Craig.'

The clouds were gathering darkly over the sea and white birds flew inland with piercing melancholy cries.

Craig grinned. 'Sandra! A chink in the independent armour at last! I thought you didn't need me in the least.'

Sandra smiled ruefully. 'Let's say I need company.'

'You'll need help too to get to the top of this high dune. Come, let's see how we can manage it.'

They struggled up the steep dune, sliding back in their tracks as often as they progressed forward. Sandra was grateful for Craig's firm hand in the small of her back. As it was when she arrived at the top her heart and lungs felt near to bursting.

And then there was nothing. No habitation, nothing to be seen but more stretches of sand and more black bushy growth.

'It's no use,' said Craig, holding Sandra firmly in the strong wind that was whipping the loose sand from the top of the dunes. 'We'll have to wait until it's light. We'd only lose ourselves if we set out now. The people at the airport will organize help tomorrow morning. I told them we'd be perfectly all right till then.'

Sandra could not help but agree. It would be

madness to go any further in the swiftly gathering night. They found their way back to the plane and Craig began to examine their equipment with the help of a torch he had had the foresight to get from the plane before it was too dark to see inside it.

'A tarpaulin, one blanket, one pillow,' he announced. 'Better than likely. It must have been provided for the use of the passenger when night flying.'

'Here's a first aid kit as well, but we'll hope we don't have to use that. Any bruises, Sandra?'

'No,' Sandra lied. She could feel a place on her thigh where something had bumped against her when they landed, but she was determined not to make a fuss about it.

'There are sleeping tablets here. I think it would be a good idea if you took one, Sandra. You can sleep in the cabin. I'll try the beach.'

By the light of the torch there seemed to be hundreds of crabs scuttling upon the sands, but Sandra did not protest at his plan. Craig grinned quizzically. 'Not one word of regret? Aren't you sorry that I'll have to sleep on the chilly beach surrounded by crabs while you rest cosily in the plane? Who knows, there might be night adders around here!'

She looked at his mischievous expression and decided to leave him to his fate. Anything rather than have him in the cabin with her for the long hours of the night.

But when he had helped her up the steps into the cabin and she saw his tall figure disappearing into the darkness she almost had second thoughts. She wrapped the blanket around her. He had insisted upon leaving it for her. The wind was chilly and Craig only had the tarpaulin and a flying jacket to keep him warm. He had been wearing a thin safari suit all day. Should she call and say he could stay here? No, she must not give him the opportunity to think she needed his company.

The sleeping tablets had made her drowsy and she slept for a couple of hours. But the effect of them could not contend with the unusual situation in which she found herself. She woke again to hear the wind howling around the cabin with the sound of hungry hyenas. A strong south-westerly gale was blowing bringing sudden sharp squalls of rain. When she heard the icy pattering of raindrops against the windscreen she could not stay hardhearted about Craig any longer. He had left a torch for her and now she shone it out into the darkness. At first she could not see him and felt completely panic-stricken alone in the cold rainy night, but a shout from underneath the plane reassured her.

'Are you all right, Sandra?'

'Yes, I think so. But the weather isn't. Come into the plane, Craig. You can't stay out there.'

He came, his dark hair plastered down by the rain. Otherwise he had kept himself fairly dry by sheltering beneath the plane and covering himself with the tarpaulin. He shook his head like a wet retriever.

'I must say it's a little warmer in here. I was beginning to feel like an early settler sheltering under his wagon.'

'Let's have the rest of the coffee and sandwiches now,' said Sandra. 'I was saving it for morning, but this is an emergency.'

'There's a small flask of brandy for medical purposes in the first aid kit. How about a drop of that in the coffee to warm us?' Craig suggested.

Sandra had been worried because in spite of his apparent toughness, Craig's spare frame seemed to be shaken every now and again by a fit of shivering, but the hot coffee and brandy seemed to help. She tucked the blanket around him.

'Hey, what is this? What about you?'

He insisted on spreading the blanket over both of them and putting his arm around her shoulders he drew her towards him. Then when she stiffened to draw back, he patted her gently. 'Not to worry. Like the brandy this is purely medicinal too. Go to sleep, Sandra. We'll keep each other warm.'

It was just getting light when she woke again. She found herself lying against Craig's broad chest, her head on his shoulder. His arms were around her, his hand touching her cheek. Drowsily she opened her eyes and found her face only inches away from the grey eyes that seemed to be watching her with a tender concern. But as she wondered whether she had only imagined this, the expression changed to one of teasing mischief.

'For such a slender girl, you're quite a weight to support all night, aren't you, Sandra?'

She drew away from him reluctant to face the hard facts of their predicament in her drowsy state. He took her chin in his hands.

'But I must say you do have the most wonderful eyes first thing in the morning – huge dark golden lakes. I feel as if I could drown in them.'

His lips came down on hers and she felt the rough touch of his unshaven chin. He seemed suddenly to become aware of this too, for he was the first to draw back.

'Sorry about that. Just a small reward, let's say, for my gentlemanly behaviour of the past night. I'll try the radio again. I expect you would like to go along the beach and have a wash and brush-up.'

She paused on the steps of the plane and watched him fiddling with the knobs of the radio apparatus.

'Do you think . . . is there any chance of being back in time for the ball tonight?'

Gary and Vi would be bitterly disappointed if she did not appear at the contest. Although she doubted very much whether she could win, it would be terrible if having gone so far she had to give up her chance of winning that much needed money.

Craig's expression altered.

'The ball, of course. I'd forgotten all about it. Is it so important that you should go on with this, Sandra?'

'More important than I can tell you, Craig.'

For without it they would have to give up the hotel. If she won, and Gary swore he thought she had a good chance of winning, their problems would be solved for the time being.

'Tell me, why is this so vital to you? The only reason I can think of why you should be willing to enter for such a contest is that that young man of yours has persuaded you that you need the money in order to marry. Is that it?'

Sandra would not reply. She did not want him to know the real reason, for if he knew it was the problem of paying for the shark nets that was worrying her, he would insist on trying to be of some help and she could not accept charity from him.

Craig sighed. 'Well, we'll do our best to get you back in time. You know I hate the idea of your parading in front of all that mob again, but as you told me before, it's no concern of mine.'

He turned away from her and became absorbed in

the radio system. It was a fine morning, the sky washed clear by last night's rain. She walked along the beach searching for a suitable place in which to wash and soon found a rock pool that was fairly deep. She glanced back, but she was hidden from the plane by a projection of rock. She had left her costume in the plane, for she had only intended to wash, but the clear pool looked very inviting. Taking off the clothes that felt as if she had been wearing them for a week, she waded in and lay upon the sandy base, her hands clutching a rock, her hair floating upon the swell of the water, for it was a tidal pool and small waves washed into it every now and again.

It was a pretty place. Red and bright green seaweed floated in ferny fronds and bright starfish clung to the rocks. Hermit crabs scuttled past her feet and small silver fishes nudged against her body. She turned and floated, gazing up at the sky that was flecked with small rosy clouds. The water was not cold in this sheltered pool. How peaceful it was here! She hated the thought of going back and facing the ordeal of the contest at the ball tonight. And yet she must if it were possible. But would she get back in time?

She had been so absorbed in her thoughts that she had not noticed Craig's tall figure striding along the beach. It was only when she heard footsteps crunching on the coarse sand behind the concealing rock that she was suddenly alarmed.

'Craig,' she called, 'don't come any further!'

'Why not?' his voice demanded, but the footsteps had halted.

'Because I'm not properly dressed.'

His laugh rang out a little sardonically.

'And you're the girl whose bikini left little to the

imagination when you were in the beauty contest! I wouldn't have thought a little thing like not being properly dressed would bother you.'

She felt a small frisson of alarm. He could hardly know how very undressed she was, for he presumably thought she had brought her costume with her. But no, for over the large rock came the two pieces of her bikini and landed in the sand beside the pool.

'There you are. Put that on and come to have a bathe in the sea. There's a gully here that looks safe. Your pool is too tame for me.'

She hastily clambered into her costume and came around the rock to find him grinning in a quite maddening fashion.

'Have a nice bathe?' he asked.

She felt so cross that she refused to join him in the gully where the waves were more boisterous. Instead she walked up the beach and dressed in the cabin of the plane, combing her hair and applying a little make-up. Craig had found a razor amongst the pilot's possessions and had plugged it into the battery. No wonder he had looked pleased with himself when he had met her on the beach, though his former swarthy appearance fitted their nickname for him. He had only needed a black patch and a red kerchief to look a real pirate, she thought.

Now she would have to wait until he had finished his bathe before she knew whether he had made contact with the airport by radio. The only trouble with having an early morning bathe, she reflected, was that it made one so dreadfully hungry. And the sandwiches were finished.

Here came Craig now, waving cheerfully.

'I could have caught a crayfish in your pool, but

thought I'd better not. It's against regulations and I don't want a heavy fine at this stage.'

Sandra's mouth watered at the idea of a freshly grilled crayfish.

'I didn't know you minded about breaking regulations,' she said quite sharply.

'Not usually, I admit, but when one of the beach rangers may arrive at any moment to fetch us I thought I'd better be cautious.'

'A ranger? You didn't tell me.'

'I haven't had a chance. You could hardly expect me to tell you when you were indulging in skinny dipping, I think it's called, in your pretty pool.'

How infuriating he was as usual!

'Well, tell me now, for heaven's sake!' she demanded.

'The airport radio office has managed to get in touch with one of the rangers. They have radio apparatus too to keep in touch with each other. He's not too far away from here and is coming to collect you in a Land-Rover. I've arranged that a car should meet you at the main road and drive you back.'

'Just me? But what are you going to do?'

'I'll stay here. They're flying some mechanics in a helicopter later on in the day. With their help we should be able to take off again. I'd be glad if you could phone Kim when you get back.'

Sandra felt a flat desolate emotion. She was to be dismissed like a child who was too much of a nuisance!

'But you didn't need to make those special arrangements for me,' she protested.

'Of course I did. Have you forgotten about the ball?'

For the moment she had. Oh, why did it have to

happen on this particular day?

Before she could stop herself she had blurted out, 'So you won't be coming to the ball?'

He smiled as if her question had been very childish, as she supposed it had. The ball that was of so much importance to herself was of small interest to him, of course.

'I can't tell you that, Sandra. It will depend on how quickly we can get out of here. Does it mean anything to you whether I'm there or not? No, don't tell me, I know the answer. It doesn't matter in the least.'

She was saved from replying by the sound of a Land-Rover roaring over the sands. In a very short while she was being driven back to have a hasty breakfast at the ranger's house before the car arrived to take her home. She had looked back at Craig's tall figure standing beside the grounded plane, but he had not even turned to wave. She felt as if she had been away for days. And in spite of herself, all interest in the ball had been lost because he would not be there.

CHAPTER TWELVE

'I KNEW you'd be all right with Craig to look after you,' said Vi. 'I told the Tremaynes so when they phoned last evening. Of course they had let me know from the airport that you were safe, but John and Louise had heard the plane was grounded and phoned for news.'

'I'm glad they knew,' said Sandra.

'And what's more, they say they've decided to come to the ball this evening. They were going to start off almost immediately after they'd phoned. Another sugar farmer was flying to the city and they made a sudden decision to come with him. Louise was so keen to see the contest. She said she was sure you were going to win.'

Louise had asked if Vi and Sandra would join them at the Casa del Sol to have dinner before the ball. It would be lovely to see her friend again so soon. It seemed everyone could come to the ball except the man she really wanted to be there. But she mustn't think of him.

Vi's blue eyes sparkled, her silky hair stood up as if electrified.

'There's something else too, but I daren't tell you for a little while. I promised not to, but I'm absolutely bursting with it.'

'Oh, Vi, you are tantalizing! Tell me at least, is it good news?'

'I hope you'll think so. We'll see. I mustn't tell you yet, because after all it might not happen.'

Sandra was mystified, but did not have much time to

ponder over Vi's secret. She would know all in good time, she supposed. And in the meantime she must get ready for the ball. But first she must phone Kim. Kim's voice sounded very young and a little timid on the phone, but she brightened up when she heard Sandra's voice and heard that her father would be home later this evening.

'I was hoping he would change his mind and take me to the ball,' she said plaintively. 'He said I was too young, but I would have loved to see you get the prize.'

'He'll be home too late for the ball, I think. And anyway, Kim, it's not at all certain that I'm going to win.'

'Of course it is. Can't I come with you and Vi, Sandra?'

'Not if your father doesn't want you to, Kim dear. Will you be all right? Who stayed with you last night?'

'Lena, one of the servants, slept near my room. Vi phoned and said I could go to her and I wanted to go, but Manoel answered the phone and said arrangements had already been made. He came to tell me about you and Craig.'

'Well, I'm sure your father will be home later to-night. But will you be all right until then?'

'Yes, I think so,' said Kim doubtfully. 'The servants are going to a party, but Craig knew about that and said he'd arranged for someone else to come.'

'If you need anything, you must phone me. Later on I'll be at the Casa del Sol, you know that.'

'I'll be all right. Have a good time at the ball, Sandra.'

Sandra felt worried when she heard Kim's desolate

little voice, but she could not interfere with Craig's arrangements.

She phoned Gary and managed to get him at his office. Was it her imagination or did he sound a little embarrassed?

'Sandra, it's great that you came down safely. Charleen has arrived, but as there seemed to be some doubt about your being here for the ball, I arranged that she should help Julie. Julie asked her to do her hair and make-up. We were sure you wouldn't mind.'

This seemed distinctly odd to Sandra. As far as she was aware Gary had hardly spoken to Julie for weeks. She was tempted to say, 'I thought it was me you wanted to win.' But she bit the words back. What did it matter? As for her appearance, she could do without Charleen. She would be herself, but try to look as good as possible.

She washed her long hair and brushed it until it shone, twisting it into a gleaming knot, then used the make-up Charleen had provided and applied just a little to enhance the even gold of her skin. She pleated the skirt of the sari as the Indian girl had shown her and tossed the glittering embroidered drape over her shoulder. The short white blouse worn underneath was low at the neck and also showed the bronzed skin of her supple waist. Vi had lent her an old necklace of garnets that glowed like rubies in their gold setting. When she looked at herself in the mirror, she knew that even without Charleen's help, she looked lovely.

'What a pity Craig won't be here,' said Vi, voicing Sandra's innermost thoughts. Would he have approved of her appearance tonight? Sandra wondered. But he would have had eyes only for Julie, who must surely be disappointed too.

'I hope you don't mind, Sandra. I promised to pick up Julie,' Gary said when they were both ready to go. Vi had said she would drive herself later when she had arranged about dinner. Of course Craig was not here to arrange that Julie should be driven to the hotel, but it was strange that she should have asked Gary to call for her. And what about Manoel? Why hadn't Julie asked him to fetch her?

Julie was looking lovely. In her deep red dress she glowed like a rose.

'Sorry about Charleen, Sandra. We thought you weren't going to arrive in time.'

'It doesn't matter in the least,' Sandra assured her. 'In fact I rather hoped you would be too late for the contest. Has Gary told you our news?'

Gary looked embarrassed.

'I haven't yet had an opportunity to tell Sandra.'

'We're going to be married just as soon as possible. What do you think of that?'

'You and Gary?' asked Sandra.

'Of course. It was always Gary I really loved, and when we met on the beach and he told me about this marvellous new job and how we'd be able to live in Johannesburg, I just had to say I'd marry him.'

'This all happened yesterday, Sandra,' Gary said, looking at the same time happy but a trifle sheepish.

'If it hadn't been for that wonderful article he wrote he wouldn't have got this job. Wasn't it lucky you got that job teaching Kim?'

'Yes, it seems like it,' said Sandra. Events had moved too quickly and she felt a little bewildered. She wanted time to sort out her ideas.

'Now if only I could win the contest we would be able to marry straight away.'

'Oh, hold on, Julie. Sandra needs the money too.'

'Not half as much as I do. Fancy spending all that lovely cash on shark nets when it could buy beautiful furniture for our flat!'

'We haven't even got one yet,' Gary protested.

'But we will,' Julie assured him.

The hotel was looking at its most splendid tonight. The foyer with its black and white tiles, tinkling fountain and modern mosaic murals was decorated with bowls of flame-coloured anthuriums, that sub-tropical flower that looks with its single waxen petal and large stamen so exotic that it is almost artificial.

Louise and John were waiting for their dinner guests on the glassed-in verandah that looked out upon the darkening sea and gave a view which encompassed miles of coastline even as far as the bluff where the gleam of a lighthouse shone out beyond the glow of the distant city.

'How lovely to see you again so soon, all safe and sound and looking absolutely exquisite!' exclaimed Louise. She herself was looking quite beautiful in a terrace dress of many colours of lilac, violet and turquoise that enhanced her fair hair and lovely skin. She insisted that Gary and Julie should join them for dinner.

'We certainly have plenty of glamour for our table,' said John to Gary, admiring the contrast of Julie's dark good looks with the fairer beauty of the other two.

'But what a pity Craig had to stay behind to see to the plane,' said Louise. 'I bet he's absolutely livid at having to miss the ball.'

Sandra thought sadly that it was no use saying to Louise that Craig had no interest in the event. She would not believe it anyway. For a moment the gilt lettering of the huge menu that the maitre d'hotel had presented to her blurred before her eyes and then with a determined effort she concentrated on the immediate present.

'Champagne cocktails,' exclaimed Julie. 'Oh, super! Now we can drink to our engagement, Gary.'

'I had ordered them to drink to Sandra's success,' said John dryly, 'but maybe that would be a little awkward now we have two potential beauty queens here, each one as lovely as the other. I'd hate to be one of the judges, wouldn't you, Gary? I've seen the other contestants, but there's no comparison. Obviously it's between you two. It's a good thing you are such firm friends.'

It was plain, thought Sandra, whom Gary would choose. He had forgotten all about his original plan and had eyes only for Julie. Really Gary was much better suited to Julie than Craig because she seemed to need someone she could bend to her will. And she and Kim could never have got on together. But what would Craig's reaction be when he came back and found that Julie had decided to marry another man? She could only guess at the depth of his feeling, for he did not betray emotion easily. Except where I'm concerned, she thought ruefully. I can always be certain that he'll disapprove of me.

'I'm far too excited to eat,' Julie declared. But she ordered quite a substantial dinner, a Chateaubriand steak shared with Gary. Louise and Sandra had langoustines, delicious small shellfish like diminutive crayfish, grilled and served with savoury rice. John ordered steak stuffed with oysters, while Vi, who had just arrived, said she would like nothing better than a plain grilled sole.

It was very busy in the dining-room, for most of the people who were going to the ball were having dinner there beforehand. Craig would not be missed here because everything was so organized it ran like clockwork. But as Sandra glanced around she wondered why Manoel was absent. On a busy evening it was part of his duties to put in an appearance and see that everything was going smoothly. But she supposed he was concerned with the last-minute arrangements for the ball and beauty contest.

When Julie had finished her crêpes suzettes, she seemed no longer interested in the dinner party. Refusing coffee, she sprang up and seized Gary by the hand.

'Come, Gary my sweet, we don't want to miss any of the dancing, do we? You don't mind if we go now, do you? Thanks for the party. See you later, Sandra.'

'Rather an abrupt departure,' commented John. 'But I'm glad they've gone. It gives us an opportunity to tell Sandra about our plans. You haven't said anything to her yet, Vi, have you?'

'No,' said Vi, 'though I don't know how I've managed to keep quiet.'

Louise turned to her old school friend, her eyes shining with friendliness. Sandra could not help thinking how different she was from Julie. How lovely it was that they had met again!

'Sandra, John has had a bright idea. He would like to buy your hotel, do some building improvements to it and run it as a quieter kind of annexe to the Casa del Sol, a place for honeymoon couples or people who want a little more peace than the big hotel provides.'

'But how can he run it in conjunction with the Casa del Sol? Craig would never consent to that.'

'Oh, I forgot you didn't know that part of the plan. John has decided to buy an interest in Craig's hotel. It was all decided when they had that business talk. He's going in with Craig. He's very impressed with his knowledge of running hotels and his bright ideas about them. He needed some way to invest his money and this is more exciting than the dull old Stock Exchange.'

'A bit more profitable too, I hope,' said John dryly.

Sandra was stunned by all this information. She turned to Vi.

'What do you think about this, darling?'

She had thought Vi would be horrified at the idea of giving up the hotel that had been almost a life's interest to her. But Vi was smiling. In her old black chiffon dinner dress, her silver hair for once smooth and wavy, she looked unusually elegant.

'I think it's a marvellous idea. It won't bring us in such a great deal of money because of all our debts and mortgages, but it means there will be enough to live on and I can take a trip to my sister in England. She's always pressing me to come and now it won't matter how long I stay.'

'And if you would consent, Sandra dear, we would like you to stay on and run the honeymoon annexe. We would give you a good salary, of course,' said Louise as if anxious that Sandra should not feel they had made their plans with no regard for her.

'Oh, no. No, I don't think I could do that!'

Sandra had spoken with unusual vehemence and there was an awkward pause. Then Louise said gently, 'I expect Sandra feels she needs to have a rest from the hotel business. Maybe she would like to apply for a post in the city for a change. Or perhaps she would like an overseas trip too. I'm sure she deserves it.'

Leave Fair Waves? Sandra was overwhelmed with shock for a few seconds and then she began to realize that this of course would be an ideal solution for her problems. Especially with regard to Craig. If she left here and if their small hotel was sold she need never meet him again and in time she hoped she would stop eating her heart out for someone who was unattainable. For the long night on the beach had clarified her feelings. She knew she loved this exasperating man who had come into her life and taken over her thoughts so that she would never again be free of him. She could not go on working in close proximity to him.

'We've sprung this on Sandra rather suddenly,' said John soothingly, for he had noticed her nervous manner. 'But Louise wanted you to know about it, Sandra, because she knew you were anxious about winning this contest.'

'And now there's no need to worry, don't you see, Sandra?' Louise joined in. 'There's no necessity now to use the money for shark nets. That will be our business. You can just go ahead and enjoy the contest for its own sake. If you win the money you'll be able to have it for yourself. Why, if you don't want to stay here it would pay for a trip around the world.'

Of course, this turn of events made the whole exercise of the beauty contest meaningless. She had gone through all this mental anguish, showing herself off to the crowd, earning Craig's hearty disapproval, and all for nothing!

But some obstinacy in her nature made her now determined to go through with it. She could not withdraw and give Craig the satisfaction of thinking she had been influenced by his opinions. Because he did not know she had entered for the contest with the sole object of winning the money to pay for their share of the shark nets. Let him think she was vain and did not mind what she did in the way of self-display. His opinion of her could hardly be worse. And soon she would have left this place for ever and need never meet him again.

When Sandra arrived in the dressing-room, Julie had already installed herself in front of the mirror with the best light and was busy repairing her make-up with the aid of Charleen.

'Oh, hello, Sandra,' Charleen greeted her, quite un-abashed at her own defection. 'You haven't made such a bad job of your make-up. If you don't mind waiting until I've done with Julie, I'll fix it up a bit better.'

'It doesn't matter,' said Sandra.

'You look a bit pale,' said Julie, who was glowing and vibrant with her new-found happiness.

'She's all right,' said Charleen. 'It depends of course what the judges go for. Sometimes they like that lady-like type. But you have a good chance too, dear,'

'I hope so. I need that money.'

'The others haven't got a hope,' said Charleen sweepingly with the confidence of an expert. 'Nice enough girls, but not a patch on you two. No, for my money, it's either you or Sandra, dear.'

I should withdraw, thought Sandra wretchedly. I've lost all interest in the contest now. And Gary naturally has lost all interest in my winning too. I owe it to him to let Julie win the contest without any competition. But it seems too late now to change my mind.

She came back again to the idea that Craig would think she had done it for his sake. No, she could not let him think she set such store by what he had said about her entering for the contest. But how she wished now she had never heard of the wretched thing.

'Did you hear about Manoel?' asked Julie, interrupting her thoughts.

'No, what about him?'

'He's gone. This morning. I always knew he was a rogue. He took the opportunity to skip off while Craig was away.'

'Whatever do you mean?'

'He's gone to join another hotel group who intend to open a new hotel further up the coast. Gary found out that it was Manoel who started the shark scare. He thinks Manoel did it in order to discredit this place and scare people away from the hotels here so that there would be more trade for the hotel combine that he was joining.'

Sandra sighed. So if it had not been for Manoel's duplicity she would not have had all the additional worry of trying to get money together for the shark nets and of trying to run a hotel that was scarcely paying its way.

She thought of John's offer that she should stay to run the honeymoon annexe. It would be child's play after the struggle with the failing Wave Crest, but she would never consider it. The money offered to Vi would only provide a small income for her after the debts and mortgages were paid off, so Sandra would have to seek some work quite soon. If only she could win the contest she could please herself what she did. She would have money to travel and get right away from everything connected with Craig. She took a sudden decision and turned to Charleen.

'Please make me look a bit brighter, Charleen. I'd

like to give Julie some competition.'

'That's the spirit! I'll do my best.'

With several deft touches, Charleen improved Sandra's appearance, fluffing out her hair and making her pale skin glow with peachy highlights, putting a new gloss over her lipstick and improving the shape of her eyebrows.

'There, now you look superb. Julie will have hard work to better that. You were my first customer I would rather you won.'

Julie had gone to the other end of the dressing-room and had been talking to the other contestants, but now she came back and was not at all pleased to see Charleen improving Sandra's looks.

'What a rat you are, Charleen! You know how much I want to win.'

'Sorry, ducky, I can't resist trying to beautify someone with as much potential as Sandra.'

There was a knock at the door and an Indian page appeared. 'Calling Miss Sandra Hamilton ... Miss Kim Ransom is on the phone.'

'Kim probably wants to wish me luck,' she said to Julie. 'I won't be a minute. Why, what's the matter?' For Julie was standing with her hand to her mouth.

'Heavens, I quite forgot! Craig asked Mum a few days ago to arrange for a sitter for Kim because the servants would be going out and he was expecting to have to attend the ball. We were supposed to pick up the sitter and take her to the house on our way here. And she isn't on the phone.' Then seeing Sandra's expression she said hastily, 'But there's no need to worry. Kim's a big girl. She'll be quite all right by herself for a little while. And you said yourself that Craig should be back soon.'

Sandra hastened to the phone at the reception desk.

'Kim, are you all right?'

'Oh, Sandra, I'm glad I got you! There's no one here but me and I'm all locked in, but I went to the kitchen to get a glass of milk and someone tried the door handle.' Her voice rose to a frightened pitch. 'I'm so scared, Sandra!'

At the reception desk there was the sound of people laughing and talking as they made their way to the ballroom. Music flooded down the curving staircase. Everywhere there was light and gaiety. But the scene was blacked out in Sandra's mind by the picture of a frightened child alone in that vast mansion that Craig had hoped would be a home for her.

'Hold on, Kim. I'll phone the police to come and find out if there's anyone around, and I'll come myself as quickly as I can get there.'

'But ... but what about the contest? Is it over yet?'

Sandra took a sudden decision. 'Yes, Kim, it's over, and I didn't win. I didn't stand a chance against Julie. I'm quite free to come.'

'Oh, I am sorry. But no, I'm not. I'm glad. If you'd won you wouldn't be able to come. Oh, please come quickly!'

They were calling her name as she ran down the steps. Vi had handed over the keys of the car to her when she arrived. Thank goodness it was parked in a place where it was easy to get out.

She drove quickly, but the police were there before her. They had picked up a vagrant who had tried the back door in the hope of getting some food. He was well known to them but harmless, they said. At

Sandra's suggestion they agreed not to make any charge but to take the man and give him a meal.

Kim, white-faced, clung to her, and did not want to let her go.

'You won't leave me now, will you? You will stay with me until Craig comes back?'

'Of course I won't leave you. I don't know about waiting for Craig, but I'll wait until Lena returns anyway.'

She stayed with Kim until she became drowsy.

'You won't go far away,' the child murmured. 'Go into Craig's room. There's a bell there connected with this room and I can call you if I wake.'

'Very well. Stop worrying, Kim. Go to sleep. If you want me I'll be there.'

The room with its gorgeous curtains and beautiful furniture still looked as unlived-in and austere as ever. She wandered into the dressing-room. Even the little photograph of Kim's mother had gone. She let herself out on to the verandah where Kim said she and Craig sometimes had breakfast. It was furnished with luxurious patio furniture and she sat on a day-bed and put her feet up.

Now that the crisis was over she was terribly tired. The exhausting events of the last two days were taking their toll. The lights sparkled on the curving coastline far into the distance and below on the beach the waves made a soft whispering sound. Kim seemed to be settled now. Although Sandra did not intend it, her eyes grew heavy from lack of rest and in a few minutes she was asleep.

But it was not a dreamless sleep. Too much had happened in too short a time. Scenes flitted before her sleeping vision, the plane and the moments before they landed upon the beach, the struggle up the sand dunes, the crowded dining-room of the hotel, and always in every confused scene there was Craig, with his teasing smile that could change to an expression of great tenderness. But in the dreams the tenderness was not for Julie or for Kim but for her, Sandra. The Craig of her dreams loved her as she knew the real one could never do.

And so when she woke to find Craig stooping over her and then kneeling to take her in his arms it seemed quite natural.

'Sandra, my dear, what are you doing here? I must say I didn't expect such a pleasant surprise.'

In her drowsy state she had returned to his embrace, putting her arms around his neck and accepting his tender kiss without drawing away. In fact she had kissed him herself before she realized that this was the real Craig and that he was not just part of her dream.

'Sandra, my sweet, how lovely you look, but what about the ball and the contest? What are you doing here?'

'Kim was alone. I had to come.'

She explained the situation, and all the time he held her just as tenderly as he had in her dream.

'So you missed the contest, and all on account of Kim?'

'Yes, but it wasn't such a sacrifice. There was no real need for the money any more now that I didn't need it for the shark nets.' She explained about Manoel's request, and how he had now gone.

'So that's what you wanted it for! Manoel had no right to ask you for the money. He's a shark himself. We're well rid of him. Now I can start afresh with John as a partner.'

'Julie is sure to have won,' said Sandra. 'It's just as well. She was so keen to win the money to buy furniture for her and Gary to set up house.'

She suddenly realized what she had said. Of course Craig did not yet know about Julie's engagement to Gary. How could she have broken it to him so abruptly!

But he was smiling.

'So they're engaged. Well, that doesn't seem a bad idea. I think young Gary is all set to go far in his profession.'

'But . . . but don't you mind?'

'Mind? About their engagement? Why should I mind?'

'But I thought . . . I thought you and Julie. . . .'

Craig laughed. 'And I thought you and Gary were all set to make a match of it.'

Sandra shook her head. 'I've never thought of Gary in that way.'

Craig's eyes were alight with teasing mischief.

'Julie's an attractive minx, but not my type. So you thought I was attracted to her and all the time I thought you were in love with Gary? Well, it seems we were both wrong. Who do you suppose I've been in love with ever since I first saw her looking so sweet in her blue bikini?'

She turned away, confused by the meaningful expression of his face. It could not be true — and yet it was.

'Of course it's you that I've loved all along, my beautiful, exasperating Sandra. How could you have thought otherwise? But all the time I thought I hadn't a chance.'

He was kissing her and this time she did not draw back, for she knew that he spoke the truth when he said she was the woman he loved. What did it matter that up to now their modes of living had differed so much? This bleak house could be transformed into a place of love and laughter, for home was where the heart was.

Why the smile?

... because she has just received her **Free Harlequin Romance Catalogue!**

... and now she has a complete listing of the many, many Harlequin Romances still available.

... and now she can pick out titles by her favorite authors or fill in missing numbers for her library.

You too may have a **Free Harlequin Romance Catalogue** (and a smile!), simply by mailing in the coupon below.

GOLDEN HARLEQUIN LIBRARY

A Treasury of Harlequin Romances!

Many of the all time favorite Harlequin Romance Novels have not been available, until now, since the original printing. But on this special introductory offer, they are yours in an exquisitely bound, rich gold hardcover with royal blue imprint. Three complete unabridged novels in each volume. And the cost is so very low you'll be amazed!

Golden Harlequin Library

Handsome, Hardcover Library Editions at Paperback Prices! ONLY $1.75 each volume.

This very special collection of 30 volumes (there'll be more!) of classic Harlequin Romances would be a distinctive addition to your library. And imagine what a delightful gift they'd make for any Harlequin reader!

Start your collection now. See reverse of this page for full details.

SPECIAL INTRODUCTORY OFFER!

Order volumes No. 1, 2, 3, 4 and 5 now and get volume No. 6 FREE!

Just imagine . . . 18 unabridged HARLEQUIN ROMANCES beautifully bound in six library editions for only $8.75.

L

M   GHL 972